When Hunter had touched Eve, so many old feelings had come rushing back along with new ones.

She'd agreed to his conditions, not only to save her inheritance, but also to rescue her dreams. Hunter had been the man of her dreams, and she hadn't realized it. When she'd met Hunter and talked with him and laughed with him and come to know the true definition of attraction, it had all taken her by surprise. *He* had taken her by surprise.

Five years ago there had been a recklessness about him that told the rest of the world to be damned because he was going to get exactly what he wanted. She'd never known recklessness or impulsiveness. He'd been a man who'd known how to take risks, and she'd been scared by that. Now she was the one taking the risk, and he seemed guarded.

Tonight they both needed time to think about this marriage of convenience—what they expected and where it could take them....

Dear Reader,

From the enchantment of first loves to the wonder of second chances, Silhouette Romance demonstrates the power of genuine emotion. This month we continue our yearlong twentieth anniversary celebration with another stellar lineup, including the return of beloved author Dixie Browning with *Cinderella's Midnight Kiss*.

Next, Raye Morgan delivers a charming marriage-of-convenience story about a secretary who is *Promoted—To Wife!* And Silhouette Romance begins a new theme-based promotion, AN OLDER MAN, which highlights stories featuring sophisticated older men who meet their matches in younger, inexperienced women. Our premiere title is *Professor and the Nanny* by reader favorite Phyllis Halldorson.

Bestselling author Judy Christenberry unveils her new miniseries, THE CIRCLE K SISTERS, in *Never Let You Go*. When a millionaire businessman wins an executive assistant at an auction, he discovers that he wants her to be *Contractually His*…forever. Don't miss this conclusion of Myrna Mackenzie's THE WEDDING AUCTION series. And in Karen Rose Smith's *Just the Husband She Chose*, a powerful attorney is reunited in a marriage meant to satisfy a will.

In coming months, look for new miniseries by some of your favorite authors. It's an exciting year for Silhouette Books, and we invite you to join the celebration!

Happy reading!

Mary-Theresa Hussey

Mary-Theresa Hussey
Senior Editor

Please address questions and book requests to:
Silhouette Reader Service
U.S.: 3010 Walden Ave., P.O. Box 1325, Buffalo, NY 14269
Canadian: P.O. Box 609, Fort Erie, Ont. L2A 5X3

JUST THE HUSBAND SHE CHOSE

Karen Rose Smith

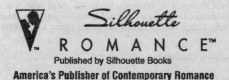

Silhouette

R O M A N C E™

Published by Silhouette Books

America's Publisher of Contemporary Romance

To Terry Himmelheber with appreciation and thanks.

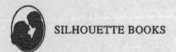 SILHOUETTE BOOKS

ISBN 0-373-19455-2

JUST THE HUSBAND SHE CHOSE

Copyright © 2000 by Karen Rose Smith

Visit Silhouette at www.eHarlequin.com

Printed in U.S.A.

KAREN ROSE SMITH

lives in Pennsylvania with her husband of twenty-nine years. Creating her two most recent books about heroes who are twins was both challenging and fun for her. She believes in happily-ever-afters, and writing about them brings her great joy. A former teacher, she now writes romances full-time. She likes to hear from readers, and they can write to her at: P.O. Box 1545, Hanover, PA 17331.

IT'S OUR 20th ANNIVERSARY!
We'll be celebrating all year,
Continuing with these fabulous titles,
On sale in June 2000.

Romance

#1450 Cinderella's Midnight Kiss
Dixie Browning

#1451 Promoted—To Wife!
Raye Morgan

 #1452 Professor and the Nanny
Phyllis Halldorson

 #1453 Never Let You Go
Judy Christenberry

 #1454 Contractually His
Myrna Mackenzie

#1455 Just the Husband She Chose
Karen Rose Smith

Desire

 #1297 Tough To Tame
Jackie Merritt

#1298 The Rancher and the Nanny
Caroline Cross

 #1299 The Cowboy Meets His Match
Meagan McKinney

#1300 Cheyenne Dad
Sheri WhiteFeather

 #1301 The Baby Gift
Susan Crosby

#1302 The Determined Groom
Kate Little

Intimate Moments

 #1009 The Wildes of Wyoming—Ace
Ruth Langan

 #1010 The Best Man
Linda Turner

 #1011 Beautiful Stranger
Ruth Wind

#1012 Her Secret Guardian
Sally Tyler Hayes

#1013 Undercover with the Enemy
Christine Michels

#1014 The Lawman's Last Stand
Vickie Taylor

Special Edition

 #1327 The Baby Quilt
Christine Flynn

 #1328 Irish Rebel
Nora Roberts

 #1329 To a MacAllister Born
Joan Elliott Pickart

 #1330 A Man Apart
Ginna Gray

#1331 The Sheik's Secret Bride
Susan Mallery

#1332 The Price of Honor
Janis Reams Hudson

Chapter One

Will you marry me?

The bold question had Eve Ruskin shaking in her black patent high heels this sunny April morning. It wasn't just the question. It was the idea of posing it to Hunter Coleburn that made her hands clammy and her heart race, never mind that she wasn't used to the higher altitude in Denver. Never mind that her life was about to take a 180-degree turn. Never mind the stipulation in her father's will that had dealt a second blow after his death.

When she pulled open the heavy glass door to the office building that housed a variety of professional firms, she saw the directory on the wall inside the lobby. She quickly crossed to it and found Hunter's name. His law practice was located on the sixth floor.

Stopping in the powder room off the lobby, she checked her makeup, the cut of her shoulder-length hair that kept her black waves manageable, and her two-piece fuchsia-and-black suit. She had to look perfect. She had to *be* perfect. She had to get this over with before she fell apart.

During her ride to the sixth floor, she vividly remembered the last time she'd seen Hunter...and the grim set of his jaw when she'd refused his marriage proposal. Five years ago at nineteen, she'd been young, inexperienced and still under her father's thumb. Since she had been protected all of her life, the idea of leaving her home and everything she'd known had terrified her. Hunter had swept her off her feet in a very short time, but she'd known little about him and had no vision of the life they might share. He'd been older, sophisticated and experienced with women. Hunter had been building a specialized practice in international law and had wanted her to leave her home in Savannah, fly to Italy with him and marry him. But the whirlwind of emotions she'd experienced had scared her as much as Hunter's intensity had. She'd told him goodbye and he'd left to build his life, his career, and to find satisfaction with another woman.

When she'd phoned his hotel in Florence...

Eve pushed aside the memory of that phone call, as well as the memories of her pregnancy and miscarriage.

A few minutes later, she stood before the glass door with Hunter's name painted on it. She stepped inside, encompassed by the feel and silent sound of luxury. The plush camel carpeting muted her footsteps as she approached the receptionist's desk.

Squaring her shoulders and lifting her chin high, she said, "I'd like to see Hunter Coleburn."

The receptionist, who looked to be in her fifties, dropped her tortoiseshell reading glasses onto their gold chain and paid attention to Eve. "I'm sorry. You must have the wrong day and time. Mr. Coleburn doesn't have any appointments this morning."

Not to be turned away when she'd come this far, Eve kept her tone calm. "I'm sure if you tell Mr. Coleburn I'm here, he'll see me. My name is Eve Ruskin."

The secretary's gaze appraised Eve again and, for the first time in her life, Eve was grateful her father had sent her to Miss Berry's Finishing School... grateful she'd been taught how to receive her father's clients with decorum, thankful her Southern breeding had taught her to be every inch a lady.

"Are you a client of Mr. Coleburn's?" the gray-haired woman asked with an arched brow.

Obviously, this was Hunter's gatekeeper, but Eve intended to speak with him this morning if she had to walk down the hall and find him herself.

"No, I'm not a client," she said without further explanation.

But the woman wouldn't give up. "And the nature of your...visit?"

"That depends on Hunter," Eve replied sweetly, using every bit of her Southern charm.

Hunter's receptionist looked startled for a moment, then recovered. "I'll see if he has a few moments," she said politely.

Though relief washed over Eve, she couldn't congratulate herself yet. She'd done some checking and found a recent article about Hunter in the style section of last month's *Denver Chronicle*. He'd been photographed with a beautiful blond woman's arm hooked through his, but there had been more than one comment about his bachelor status. He wasn't married, yet that didn't mean he wasn't involved with someone...maybe even the blonde, whose fashion company had hired him to do their legal work overseas.

The receptionist lifted the receiver on the console to her right and pressed a button. Then she said, "There's a woman to see you, Mr. Coleburn. Her name is Eve Ruskin."

Eve's heart pounded in her ears.

After a few moments, the receptionist frowned and hung up the phone. "He said to send you back. It's the last door on the left."

With a smile and a "thank you," Eve clutched her purse much too tightly and walked down the hall. The decor of the office suite was burled walnut, forest-green and shades of brown. The first office door stood open and Eve glimpsed a woman, probably in her twenties, wearing a headset. She was transcribing. The second door was labeled Conference Room. Across from it was a space that looked very much like a living room, with its leather couches and chairs and occasional tables. There was a bathroom next door.

Finally Eve stood in front of Hunter's office. She'd lost her spirit after her miscarriage. But her father's death had made her reassess her life. She was going to forge a new course. The question was whether she had the nerve to forge it with Hunter and whether enough time had passed that he could forgive her. The hardwood door was half open, and she stepped inside.

Hunter was seated at a massive desk with folders and papers spread all around him. His black leather chair was high-backed, and his white dress shirt was a contrast against it. He wore a black-and-robin-egg-blue silk tie, and when he looked up from the folder in front of him, her heart almost stopped. His coal-black hair was parted on the side and swept casually over his brow. His face was ruggedly handsome and tanned, and she remembered he liked to ski when he could. Of course, he might have picked up that tan on the French Riviera, too. But what she noticed most was the remoteness in his blue eyes and the lack of expression on his face.

"Hello, Hunter."

When he pushed back his chair and rose to his feet, she thought he might come around the desk to greet her. But he didn't. He stood tall and silent, appraising her in one long look.

"Hello, Eve."

The silence that stretched between them was hers to break. "I suppose you're wondering why I'm here."

He motioned to one of the two wood-and-leather chairs in front of his desk and waited until she was seated before he lowered himself again into his seat. "Yes, I am."

Even with the massive desk between them, Eve could feel the visceral pull toward Hunter. It had been there from the moment she'd met him. Logic had told her the years would have made a difference. They were different people now and they'd both changed. Yet the only change in Hunter seemed to be the faint lines around his eyes, those creasing his forehead. When he'd stood, she'd seen that he was as sleek and muscled as ever, maybe more so. At thirty-two now, he was in his prime, and it showed.

Renewing her resolve, holding on to her courage, she asked, "Will you marry me?"

Silver sparked in Hunter's blue eyes, but only for a moment. "I think you'd better explain." His low, calm voice rattled her completely.

She rushed into an explanation. "My father died three months ago." Her voice caught, but she pushed on. "He put a stipulation in his will that if I don't marry within a year, everything in his estate will be donated to charity."

The silence was palpable until Hunter asked, "And why did you choose me?"

Was that interest in his eyes? Did they have a chance to recapture what they'd once had? Had he never married for a reason? The same reason she'd never looked at another man? "The truth is, Hunter, there aren't any men I...know well enough to ask."

At that, his brows arched. "What about that land developer, Jerry Livingston?"

"Jerry and I weren't suited for each other. I convinced Father of that long before he died." Actually it had been her lack of zeal in anything but her studies in art history, earning her degree, and then her position at the art museum in Savannah that had convinced her father she would probably never marry.

Hunter leaned forward and propped one arm on his desk. "What makes you think I'd consider your proposal?"

She could feel the heat in her cheeks, but she kept her chin up. If any remnant of what he'd once felt for her remained, he was hiding it well.

Before she'd purchased her ticket to Denver, she'd realized she'd have to give Hunter a tangible reason to entertain the idea of marriage. "This can be a business arrangement. If you marry me, the art collection that you admired and my father treasured will be yours."

Deep down she was hoping that if Hunter agreed to this, as they talked and consulted about the estate, maybe they could establish a connection again, maybe she could tell him about the miscarriage, maybe she could tell him she'd made a mistake so many years ago.

But his deep voice gave nothing away as he responded, "I see."

She held her breath and waited.

"Give me twenty-four hours." He took a card from the wood-and-brass holder on his desk. Standing, he held it out to her. "Come to my penthouse tomorrow evening, and I'll give you my decision."

As she stood and reached for his card, her fingertips brushed his and an almost electric charge ran through her. Gazing up at his face, she tried to see if he'd been affected, too, but she couldn't tell. Maybe he held no memories of their interlude five years ago. Maybe he had only regrets.

She tucked the card into her purse. "Is seven o'clock all right?"

"Make it eight. Sometimes I get tied up here. I'll call you if I hit a snag. Where are you staying?"

"The Mountain Inn."

He nodded, and she knew that the nod was a dismissal.

Turning, she walked to the door and then stopped. "It's good to see you again, Hunter."

When he didn't respond, she opened the door and

stepped out into the hall. She made it to the lobby, then she sank down onto one of the wrought-iron benches and realized she was shaking all over. Emotions she'd tamped down for years overwhelmed her. She obviously still felt a great deal for Hunter Coleburn, but it was a mystery as to what he felt for her.

Shell-shocked, Hunter watched his office door close. Memories from five long years ago broke through the dam he'd constructed and flooded his mind as he sank heavily into his desk chair. He swore, then went over his conversation with Eve again in his head, hearing her soft Southern accent, still inhaling the gardenia scent of her perfume....

For a moment when she'd entered his office, the years had slipped away. Then he'd recalled her refusal to marry him and the pain of leaving her. No sooner had he laid eyes on her again than his body had remembered as well as his mind. She aroused him as no other woman ever had. Today he'd resented that fire-in-his-blood feeling. He had to admit she was more sophisticated and confident now than she'd been five years ago. It had taken a lot of guts for her to come here and propose to him.

Then again, maybe not. If this was merely a business arrangement she was proposing...

Glad for the distraction when his phone rang, Hunter snatched it up. Eve's appearance in his office had unsettled him more than he wanted to admit, and he had to consider very carefully everything she'd said. Yet when his receptionist told him his sister, Jolene Morgan, was on the line, he realized the day held more than one surprise.

Hunter's relationship with his adoptive family was complicated. He'd always felt like an outsider, as if blood *was* thicker than a decree that had made him John and Martha Morgan's son.

"Hunter, do you have a few minutes?" Jolene asked. Unlike their brother Larry, she was always friendly.

"Sure, what's up?"

"It's Dad."

To further complicate his relationship with his family, this past Christmas Hunter had learned he'd been separated from his twin brother, Slade. They'd reunited a few months ago after Slade's search had led him to Hunter. In the process, as the whole story unfolded, Hunter had learned that Martha and John Morgan had taken him from the orphanage but had left Slade behind. He couldn't seem to shake the anger that had accompanied that revelation.

Still, he cared about his adoptive parents deeply. "What's wrong?"

"I'm not sure, but Mom says he's not sleeping at night and he's having indigestion all the time. I think it has to do with Larry taking over the business when Dad retires next year."

Ever since they were kids, Larry had done everything he could to ingratiate himself with their parents. Hunter had realized early on that Larry was the golden one, the "real" son. John Morgan's pride in Larry's accomplishments seemed greater. He'd always taken a more hands-off approach with Hunter, so Hunter had decided to set his own course. That's why he'd gone into law instead of assuming a position at Morgan's Office Products.

"Have you talked to Larry about this?" Hunter asked.

"He says I should stop worrying so much, that nothing's wrong with Dad that retirement won't fix. But I'm not so sure. Will you talk to Dad?"

"Jolene…"

"I know things have been strained between you for the past few months, but I think he'll tell you what's really going on."

Hunter hadn't stopped by his parents' house lately. He'd spent a few days with them in January while he was recuperating from the accident that had brought him face-to-face with Slade. But since then, between working late and business trips—"I'll stop in over the weekend and see what I can find out."

"Thanks, Hunter. And you'll let me know?"

"I'll let you know."

After he said goodbye to Jolene, he stood and crossed to the windows and looked down onto the busy Denver street.

For the past five years, he'd concentrated on nothing but work. He'd been determined to make his law practice a success. He'd worked to find his place in the world. He'd worked to forget about Eve.

And now she was in Denver asking him to marry her.

This would be a *business arrangement,* she'd said.

Hunter thought about all the years Larry had purposefully shut him out. He thought about his feelings of separateness from the rest of the family and how he'd taken back the Coleburn name when he was twenty-one. He thought about being reunited with his twin brother, and Slade's marriage shortly after. He thought about how happy Slade and his wife Emily seemed to be.

What if he told Eve that a business arrangement wasn't enough, that he wanted a family instead? She might fly right back to Savannah. But if her inheritance meant enough to her, perhaps she wouldn't.

Tomorrow night he'd find out.

When Eve stepped into Denver's poshest apartment building, the uniformed security guard asked her name. She gave it, and then he asked her for a photo ID. After she showed him her driver's license, he smiled and handed her what looked like a magnetic hotel-room key, explaining it was for the penthouse suite. She had to insert it in the elevator to be able to reach the top floor.

Eve had known luxury in her life, but it was an old-fashioned, country kind of luxury that came from generations of Ruskins who'd left behind not only their wealth, but items they treasured. She didn't care about her father's money. She earned a modest salary working at the art gallery and that was all she required. But her father had known there were treasures in his estate that she wouldn't want to part with—her mother's jewelry, items in the house that held memories of her mother and her childhood. Of course, she also appreciated his collection of paintings. They were one of the reasons she'd majored in art history in college. But she knew Hunter appreciated them as well. And if he helped her save the rest, she'd be happy.

Happy.

It was a word with a wispy definition. One you could never quite grasp. She didn't know why her father had done this to her, but she suspected his lawyer knew. After he'd read the will, the elderly man had patted her on the shoulder and said she would understand in time.

She understood only that she couldn't lose her past, her roots, her last memories of both her parents. If she had reminders of them, she could hold on to those memories more securely.

As the elevator ascended to the twentieth floor, Eve straightened her short turquoise jacket, brushing a piece of lint from the matching linen dress underneath. Her stomach had been topsy-turvy all day, and she reminded herself that she was scared. What if Hunter said *no?* What if Hunter said *yes?*

Taking a deep calming breath, she stepped out of the elevator when it stopped and pressed the bell on Hunter's doorjamb. She was fifteen minutes early. The door didn't open immediately and Eve wondered if Hunter had gotten tied up at his office, if he'd tried to reach her and she hadn't gotten the message.

After what seemed like an interminable wait, Hunter opened the door and a soft gasp escaped her lips. He was wearing black jogging shorts and running shoes and nothing else. The breadth of his shoulders, all of that tanned, taut skin, the black curling hair running down the center of his chest, made her breathless and she couldn't seem to find her voice.

"You're early," he said, neither critically nor enthusiastically. "I was hoping to finish my workout before you arrived. Come on in. I'll get a quick shower, then we can talk."

When he dropped back a pace so she could enter, their gazes locked. There was an electric awareness there. They'd once made passionate love, and the images shimmered between them like tangible ghosts. Hunter's scent was like an intoxicating wave, and the virile power of his body beckoned to her.

Breaking eye contact, she moved into his apartment.

Forcing herself to concentrate on her surroundings, she found sleek dark pine, brass, navy-and-green plaids on the sofa and a comfortable-looking armchair. Deep green draped the windows, framing the magnificent view of the city. The carpet was also deep green with flecks of navy. Lights from other buildings twinkled in the April dusk and Eve supposed that at night the view was as impressive as the New York skyline.

"Make yourself comfortable," Hunter said politely. "I'll only be ten minutes."

Then he disappeared down a hall, and a few moments later she heard a shower running. Imagining his hair slick and wet, his body naked... Shaking the image away, she crossed to the entertainment center and studied his collection of CD's, remembering he liked the sultry sound of jazz. They'd gone to a jazz club in Savannah one night.

Less than ten minutes later, Hunter returned to the living room wearing a tan polo shirt and khaki slacks with loafers. Even though he was dressed now, he was still disturbingly male.

Approaching her, he stopped only a few inches away. "You know, don't you, that if I consent to this marriage, it will be everything your father didn't want for you. He wanted a man with a pedigree. I don't have one. Worse than that, I was probably a bastard. No father was named on my birth certificate. You come from a line of blue bloods. All I have from who-ever my ancestors were is the Coleburn name."

There was pain in Hunter's eyes as he admitted what he saw as truth.

"I don't care about any of that," she responded with certainty.

"No, what you care about is finally rebelling against your father and not losing your inheritance."

"I'm not rebelling."

"Then why not choose a man from your father's country-club set?" Hunter fired back.

"Because I don't know any of them." The word *know* as it was defined in the biblical sense rang be-tween them.

His brows rose as if he didn't believe her. "Who escorted you to your father's parties, to the theater, to the doings at the 'club'?"

When she was nineteen, all of those things were part of her life. Since Hunter and her miscarriage, she'd cut them out. "Father didn't entertain much the past few years. I've spent my time working at a museum and helping in the pediatrics ward at the hospital." Hunter's blue gaze was so penetrating she thought he might be able to see the corner of her heart where she'd secreted away her feelings for him.

"Before I give you an answer to the question you posed yesterday, you'll have to consent to an experiment."

She took a shallow breath. "What kind of experiment?"

His voice went low as he murmured, "This." His arms surrounded her and before she could blink, he'd set his lips on hers.

Magic.

Hunter Coleburn's kiss was as magical and fantastic as she'd remembered it. His lips were firm and hot...so expert...so coaxing. Chaste pressure gave way to his tongue parting her lips. He swept her into erotic sensations with a stroke and a thrust and a thorough exploration that sent flashes of heat throughout her body. She couldn't think. She could only feel...and want...and remember.

As abruptly as he'd begun the kiss, he ended it and stepped back.

Opening her eyes, she found her balance on her high heels and clasped her hands in front of her to still their trembling.

"If I consent to marry you, I have a few conditions," he stated as if the kiss had never happened.

Finding her voice, she asked, "And they are...?"

"We would have a real marriage and live in Denver."

A *real* marriage. To him that meant... From the look in his eyes she knew what that meant—sharing a bed. And if she moved to Denver, she'd have to sell her family home. But if she didn't marry Hunter, it would be sold anyway.

"And I'd like to start a family as soon as possible," he added.

He wanted a family. That thought made her heart swell with an ache that had been there since her miscarriage. She should tell him about the pregnancy and miscarriage, but she couldn't. Not yet. Not until she felt some emotional connection to him again. Before she'd come to Denver, she'd had a thorough checkup with the doctor who had treated her after she'd lost their baby. As he had five years ago, he'd told her once more that there was no reason she couldn't get pregnant again and have healthy children.

Hunter's jaw had set firmly as she thought about his conditions, and his voice was almost bitter now as he studied her. "I know you're not an impulsive woman, Eve. If you need to think about it—"

Once before she'd had too many doubts, and her confusion had cost her a life with Hunter. *She'd* come to *him*, and she wasn't going to hesitate this time. She was going to take a risk.

"I don't need to think about it. I accept your conditions." Was that relief in his eyes? Maybe something more?

"Well, then," he concluded, "why don't we move you in tonight?"

Chapter Two

"You want me to move in tonight?" Eve asked, stunned.

"Is there any reason why you shouldn't?"

Hunter himself had been surprised when he'd said the words. Yet if he and Eve were going to get married, they might as well get used to being around each other. As he'd thought about the idea of marriage and having a family of his own, accepting her proposal had made more and more sense. Along with the desire that ran rampant whenever he was in the same room with her was the sense of completing something that had never been finished.

"Do you expect me to…?" She stopped, her cheeks reddening. "I mean, where will I stay?"

"I have a guest room. As I said, I want this to be a real marriage. But we can wait till our wedding night to consummate it."

She didn't seem to know what to say to that. She

looked nineteen again, unsure, and he wondered if she regretted ever coming to him.

"Having second thoughts?" he had to ask. Maybe he shouldn't have made his acceptance sound so cut-and-dried. But looking at her, still wanting her with the fiery need he'd experienced five years ago, he realized the pain of her refusal had never diminished. He wouldn't let himself step into the quicksand of caring too much again.

"No, I'm not having second thoughts. I just...I guess I didn't expect things to happen so fast. I thought we might take some time to get to know each other again."

"I knew you once, Eve, and I don't think people change that much in the course of a lifetime. If you intend to marry to resolve your legal tangle, then it's best we don't wait."

She looked as if she was debating with herself. "I have to return to Savannah to sort through my father's belongings and put the house on the market."

He remembered how she'd loved that house, how tradition and roots were as important to her as they were to her father. Selling her family home was going to be difficult for her. "My schedule's flexible for the next few weeks. Let's go pick up your things, then we can discuss how we want to go about the arrangements."

"I only have a suitcase and a garment bag, Hunter. I can get them myself."

In spite of what he believed about people changing, he could see some differences in Eve. She was still a Southern beauty, but she wasn't a protected, sheltered young woman any longer. She'd always had spirit, but now it shone more clearly in her beautiful gray eyes. "All right. While you're gone, I'll call my real estate agent and ask her to fax me some listings."

"Listings?"

"Sure. The city's been fine, but I've been thinking about buying a house."

"Maybe you should wait."

"Until…?"

Her hands floated in front of her. "At least until after we're married."

"It won't hurt to look. It might take us a while to find what we want."

He couldn't seem to take his eyes off hers, and the desire to pull her into his arms again was so strong he could taste it. But he remembered her doubts so many years ago, her refusal to marry him and build a life with him. She'd proposed a business arrangement to secure her inheritance. Marrying him was simply a means to an end. He'd better remember that.

Moving away from her, he went to the phone on the table beside the sofa. "I'll call Fred and tell him to give you a permanent key to the penthouse when you come back with your bags. He'll have someone waiting at the curb to help you with them."

She looked as if she wanted to protest, but she didn't. Instead, she picked up her purse lying on the coffee table and went to the door. "I'll see you in a little while."

He nodded.

When the door closed behind her, he raked his hand through his hair. He'd put at least twenty-four hours of analysis into this decision.

It was the right one.

* * *

Hunter called his real estate agent. She told him she'd gather information on listings tonight and fax them in the morning.

Then he paced.

What if Eve changed her mind? Even though this was her idea, she might not have thought about all the repercussions. And with his conditions... Dammit, he wanted a family, a family where he truly belonged.

When he and Slade had reunited, he'd known he'd found a true bond. But after wandering for most of his life, Slade had found a home on a ranch in Montana with Emily, her son, Mark, and her newborn daughter, Amanda. When Hunter had flown out for Slade and Emily's wedding, he had seen Slade with Mark and realized how much he wanted children of his own. Any child of his would know he was special. He'd always know he was cherished. He would always know he belonged.

Crossing to the windows, Hunter looked down on the city, now almost dark. Eve had come to him with a business arrangement. Why him? Why hadn't she married Jerry Livingston, a man handpicked by her father? Livingston had been one of the main reasons she'd refused Hunter.

A corporate attorney himself, Emory Ruskin had summoned Hunter, a specialist in international law, to his home in Savannah to deal with a client who wanted to buy a German-based business. Ruskin had hired Hunter only because he was less expensive than well-known firms who provided the same service.

One evening after Hunter had been out with Eve, Ruskin had called him to his den. Once there, in no uncertain terms he'd told Hunter that he'd be announcing his daughter's engagement to Livingston at Christmas, and she'd have everything he dreamed of for her. He'd planned his daughter's life, and he didn't want anyone tampering with those plans. Eve would show Hunter around the city, but if he had anything else in mind, he should get it out of his head.

Hunter had never liked taking orders or accepting ultimatums, and after he and Eve couldn't contain their desire and had made love, he'd asked her to fly away with him and marry him. But she'd been trained by her father and trained well. Emory Ruskin had set her course and her dreams for her, and she hadn't been strong enough or cared enough to break free of the tentacles that bound her.

Over the years, Hunter had tried to put her out of his head. He'd dated plenty of women, as well as bedded them, but he'd never gotten Eve out of his system. His experimental kiss had proved all the fire was still there. Now, besides the fire and physical satisfaction, he'd have the hope of children.

He was still staring out the window when his doorbell rang. Opening his door, he found Eve and a young man who did odd jobs around the building. He motioned them inside. "Did Fred give you the key?" he asked.

She nodded.

"Then you don't have to ring the bell." He motioned to the young man. "You can put the bags in here." After tipping the boy handsomely, he found Eve standing at the windows, looking out.

"This is a wonderful view," she said softly. "Are you sure you want to give it up?"

"I'm ready to trade the sky and city lights for the sky and trees and space."

He thought about joining her at the windows, but he knew if he did, the twinkling lights and dark sky might create an intimacy she wasn't ready for. Maybe he wasn't, either. So he gestured to the sofa. "Let's talk about the wedding. I'd like to get married here in Denver. Is that a problem?"

He waited until she came over and sat, then he lowered himself beside her.

"It's not a problem. I don't have any relatives in Savannah, just a few friends."

"A few?" Again he remembered Ruskin's circle...the calls Eve had taken while he'd stayed at the house. She'd been a social butterfly.

"Yes, a few. But I can see them when I return to Savannah. I know your family is here."

"Would you like to use a justice of the peace or a minister?" Hunter asked.

"I know it's short notice, but I'd prefer a minister and a church."

He tilted his head and studied her. A minister would mean she would be taking their ceremony seriously. "I'll see what I can do. I'd like to keep it small. There are a few friends and colleagues besides family I should invite. We'll have a reception afterward."

"Can that be arranged so quickly?" she asked.

"Anything can be arranged if you know the right people."

"Hunter, about the expenses. My inheritance is tied up until after we marry. I'll be glad to compensate you for half of everything then."

"Your inheritance is your money, Eve. I don't need

it or want it. I'll take care of the wedding and the reception. We can fly to Savannah afterward. Do you think a week will be enough there?''

"If it's not and you need to return to Denver, I can stay longer."

He frowned, thinking of the next few weeks and the basis he'd be laying for their marriage. "Then we'd better look for a house in the next few days. Can you think of anything we haven't covered?''

Her perfume teased him. It reminded him of a summer garden in Savannah, sweet with a hint of the erotic, and when she murmured, "At the moment, it all seems so overwhelming,'' he leaned slightly closer to her.

"You're in a strange city with a new life before you. That can be overwhelming. My mother will probably want to help with the arrangements. Is that a problem?''

Eve's eyes glowed with a glistening softness. "No, not at all. I'm looking forward to meeting her and the rest of your family. You have a brother and a sister, right?''

"Yes, I do. And there's someone else now, too. Around Christmas, I found out I have a twin brother. His name's Slade.''

"How wonderful! Is he here in Denver?''

"No. He lives in Montana with his new wife and her son and daughter, and I don't know if they'll be able to come to the wedding on short notice. They have a ranch that needs a lot of care. But if not at the wedding, you'll meet them soon. We'll make a point of it.''

Suddenly Eve looked troubled. After a few moments, she asked, "What are you going to tell your family? About our marriage, I mean."

"I don't have to tell them anything."

"Surely they'll wonder why you suddenly decided—"

"My family isn't that involved with my life, and I'm not involved in theirs." Every time he thought about how his parents had separated him from Slade, how they'd left his twin, resentment welled up. He didn't know if it would ever go away. "But I might tell Slade the truth, if that's not embarrassing for you."

Blushing, she looked down in her lap. "He'll probably wonder what kind of woman I am."

The opinions of others had mattered to Emory Ruskin, and they mattered to his daughter. That hadn't changed. Reaching out, Hunter slid his hand along her cheek and nudged her face toward his. "To save your inheritance, you need a husband. To start a family, I need a wife. Slade and Emily won't make any judgments, and no one else needs to know."

Eve's skin was a beautiful ivory and just as soft as he remembered. Her gray eyes sparked with a desire that made his body thrum. Yet he dropped his hand and leaned away. A sense of self-preservation even stronger than desire warned him to use caution and reminded him she could still change her mind.

She brushed her hair behind her ear and then stood. "I'd better unpack."

He stood, too. "Let me give you a tour so you know where everything is. I'll be leaving for the office early tomorrow morning, but there's no reason you have to get up. I'll call you once I find out about the availability of churches and reception halls.''

"Hunter, I don't want you to have to do everything.''

"Not everything. I'm just going to get the ball rolling. Come on, I'll show you the guest room.''

When Eve opened the closet door, she saw a fluffy, green terry robe hanging on a hook inside. Hunter's guest room, with green-and-beige-striped spread and drapes, double-sized bed, dresser and chest, had its own bathroom. Hunter had given her a quick tour of the small dining room, kitchen, gym and office. He'd opened the door to the master suite, and she'd glanced in briefly. She'd felt a funny, curling sensation in her stomach when she thought about sharing it with him.

Eve hung her dresses in the closet and wished she could get a better grasp on the turmoil inside her. Her decision to ask Hunter to marry her had started it. The twenty-four hours in which she'd waited for his answer had kept it going. And now...she should feel relieved.

He was being polite, almost friendly, and when he'd kissed her and touched her, so many old feelings had come rushing back along with new ones. But she had the feeling Hunter's definition of a real marriage included sex, and her definition included so much more. Yes, she wanted to save her inheritance, but she'd come to Hunter because...

Because she still had feelings for him? Because she wanted his forgiveness? Because she expected to pick up where they had left off?

She'd agreed to his conditions, not only to save her

inheritance, but also to save her dreams. Hunter had been the man of her dreams, and she hadn't realized it. Or maybe she had and understood that her dreams were very different from her father's. When she'd met Hunter, and talked with him and laughed with him and come to know the true definition of attraction, it had all taken her by surprise. *He* had taken her by surprise.

Five years ago there had been a recklessness about him that told the rest of the world to be damned because he was going to get exactly what he wanted. She'd never known recklessness or impulsiveness. He'd been a man who'd known how to take risks, and she'd been scared by that. Now she was the one taking the risk, and he seemed guarded.

Was he that way only with her? Had she done that to him?

As if it were yesterday, Eve remembered making the call to Florence six weeks after Hunter had left Savannah.

The phone had rung only one time before a woman had answered. "Allo." The voice had been soft and husky.

Eve had taken a deep breath. "I'd like to speak to Hunter Coleburn."

"I'm sorry," the woman had said. "He's in the shower. Would you like to leave a message?"

Eve had imagined Hunter not getting the message. She had imagined exactly what had gone on in that hotel room before Hunter's shower. It was eight o'clock in the evening in Italy, and she suspected that Hunter's night had just gotten started. From their love-making, she'd known he was a man with strong needs, and she'd been afraid of that, along with everything else.

With that phone call, she'd realized none of it mattered. Apparently Hunter had easily found someone else. Apparently he'd already put her in his past, and she decided to do the same with him by responding to the voice on the line, "There's no message." She'd hung up, resolving to raise her child alone.

But she'd miscarried two weeks later...after she'd told her father about the pregnancy, after she'd seen the deep disappointment in his eyes, after her affair with Hunter had changed her relationship with her father forever.

Trying to push the pain back into the past, she put her garment bag in the closet, then opened the suitcase on the bed. She'd stuffed in a little bit of everything, not knowing what she'd need. Going to the top drawer of the chest, she opened it and returned to the suitcase, piling panties and bras into her arms.

But when she returned to the drawer, something in the corner caught her eye. Dumping her clothes in, she picked up a red silk chemise nightgown. She could smell perfume emanating from it, strong and potent. Apparently Hunter's last guest had left it. The woman in the picture with him? Someone else?

Eve thought about Hunter's lifestyle. He had money. He traveled everywhere. He could have any woman he wanted. Would he be faithful to her? He said he wanted a family. Surely that meant he wanted commitment. They'd have to talk about it. But for tonight they both needed time to think about this marriage of convenience—what they expected and where it could take them.

They'd talk about all of it tomorrow.

* * *

The Morgans' home in a suburb of Denver was a modest two-story neatly landscaped with a hedge along one side. When Hunter had called Eve at noon, he'd asked her if she wanted to go to his parents' house for dinner, after taking a look at a church in the neighborhood where they could have their wedding. It would be available Tuesday evening for the service.

She'd loved the feel of the small church as soon as they'd stepped inside. It had a quiet holiness about it, and the minister had greeted them warmly, telling Hunter how much he respected John and Martha Morgan and the volunteer work they did at the church. Now as she and Hunter stepped inside his parents' house, she wondered what the Morgans would be like, if Hunter's environment had shaped him as a man more than his genes. She suspected that would be true but didn't know if Hunter would admit it. He'd told her long ago that he'd always felt "adopted." Eve wondered why and if his parents were the cause.

Martha Morgan was a plump woman with a big smile. She wore an apron over her short-sleeved, shirt-waisted, flowered dress and opened her arms to Eve. "We are so glad the two of you could come to dinner tonight. When Hunter phoned with his news, we were a bit...flabbergasted."

A receding hairline made John Morgan's face look longer than it actually was. After Martha's hug, he extended his hand to Eve and his brown eyes looked her over curiously. "It's a pleasure to meet you, my dear. Welcome to the family."

As Eve studied the couple, she felt they meant their

warm words. "Thank you for inviting us. We stopped at the church. It's lovely."

Martha hooked her arm into Eve's and pulled her along to the kitchen. "Come tell me everything you're thinking about for the wedding while I get supper on the table. If Hunter wants this to happen on Tuesday, we don't have much time."

Eve glanced over her shoulder at her soon-to-be husband. "Hunter..."

He gave a casual shrug. "Mom knows what she's doing. I'm sure whatever you two decide will be fine."

Martha talked as she walked, drawing Eve along with her. They went through the dining room with its maple table and chairs and huge hutch into a homey kitchen done in red-and-white gingham. The cupboards were knotty pine, the floor was shiny white linoleum, crisscrossed with black lines. "Hunter insisted he doesn't want to use the social hall at the church for the reception. He intends to invite colleagues."

"That's right. He told me he rented a reception room at the Rocky Ridge Hotel."

"It's the finest hotel in Denver," Martha said as she took her arm from Eve's and motioned to a stool at the eat-in counter.

"Can I do something to help?"

Martha gave her an approving glance. "If you'd like. Salad fixings are in the bowl, plates are in the cupboard above it."

Eve went to the counter and opened the cupboard.

"The hotel kitchen will cater the reception, but I thought maybe tomorrow you and I could go to the florist and then to the bakery to pick out a wedding cake." After Martha lifted a lid on the stove to check the steaming vegetables, she turned to Eve. "Unless you'd rather do it yourself?"

"Oh, no, I'd like you to come along. And if you have the time, maybe you could help me look for a wedding dress."

Martha's eyes misted. "I'd love to have that honor. Larry's wife and her parents pretty much planned their wedding. And I don't know if Jolene will ever get married. She puts in so many hours at that ad agency."

Taking a pot from the stove, Martha set it on a hot pad on the counter. "Hunter tells me both your parents are deceased. Your father, just recently. I'm sorry."

"He had high blood pressure for some time, but the stroke was unexpected."

"Hunter says that with no brothers and sisters, you have the responsibility of closing up the house and selling it."

Eve nodded. "That's why we're going to Savannah next week."

"How did you and Hunter meet? He didn't mention that."

"It was almost five years ago when he was doing some work for my father in Savannah."

"Then this wedding isn't as sudden as it seems."

Not sure what to say to that, Eve gathered up three dishes of salad. "Should I take these to the dining room?"

Martha gave her a quizzical look and answered, "Sure. And you can call the men to the table."

Once Martha brought steaming platters of meat, potatoes and vegetables to the dining room, a silence settled over the group. But she broke it and addressed Hunter. "Did you call Slade?"

"He and Emily can't come on such short notice."

"That's a shame," John murmured and glanced at his son.

A look passed between them that Eve didn't understand. Trying to keep the conversation flowing, she commented, "Hunter told me he and Slade just found each other recently."

An uncomfortable silence fell over the table once more, but again Martha jumped in. "Yes. Slade put an ad in the paper, and we answered it and then contacted Hunter. He was overseas at the time."

Eve looked over at Hunter. "Did you go to Montana, or did Slade come here?"

"Slade came here."

"You two weren't dating then?" John Morgan asked.

"No," Hunter said simply without further explanation.

At John's surprised look, Martha patted her husband's hand. "They met five years ago, honey. They've known each other a long time."

"I see." John addressed Eve. "Hunter gave us quite a scare when he came home from England in January. It was icy. His plane ran off the runway and he ended up in the hospital with a severe concussion and a broken leg. Did he tell you that?"

"No!"

"We called Slade, and he came to the hospital. He was there when Hunter woke up."

The undercurrent between Hunter and the Morgans was so strong it tugged at Eve, too. There was a lot more to this story than either Hunter or his parents were revealing. In time, maybe she'd understand what was going on. In time, maybe she'd understand the man she was going to marry. There had been no opportunity to talk earlier. Her pregnancy and miscarriage weren't something she just wanted to blurt out. And she needed privacy to ask him about other women in his life. She would need some answers before they went any deeper into this.

Remembering Jolene's request, Hunter took the opportunity after dinner to talk to his father. Eve and his mother were busy in the kitchen, and Hunter suspected decisions about the wedding would slow down the after-dinner cleanup. Following his father into the living room, he sat on the sofa across from the older man's recliner. Then he asked, "Are you getting ready for retirement?"

With a slight shake of his head, his father said, "Not quite yet."

Hunter decided there was no way to skate around this subject delicately. "Jolene tells me you haven't been feeling quite up to par."

"She worries too much. I'm fine."

"Sleeping and eating okay?"

His father gave Hunter a pensive look. "With retirement coming on, I'm thinking about all the things I have to do before I leave the business in Larry's hands. Sometimes that keeps me awake at night."

"But you're feeling okay otherwise?"

"I had a checkup two months ago, and I'm as fit as a fiddle. Don't let Jolene start you worrying, too."

The two men were silent for a moment then John said, "Hunter, I know there's been a strain between you and your mother and I ever since you found out about Slade."

His mother and father had explained exactly what had happened so many years ago. They hadn't been able to get pregnant, and had looked into adopting. After they were approved, the boys' home had told them they had twin eight-month-old babies who needed a family. John and Martha had decided to take the twins, but then several things happened at once. Slade contracted pneumonia and had to be hospitalized. John received a job offer from a company in Billings, Montana, that he felt would benefit his family. And Martha discovered she was pregnant. John's job had required him to relocate within a month, and in the hospital, Slade wasn't responding to treatment.

Medical bills mounted. The Cromwell Boys' Home told the Morgans they couldn't let them adopt Slade under these conditions. With a budget that was already tight and another new baby on the way, Martha and John had decided to just adopt Hunter. The orphanage assured them they would place Slade when he was well. In the weeks that followed, the Morgans had put Hunter's twin out of their minds as they concentrated on the family they were building as well as a new life far from Tucson, Arizona.

Part of Hunter had understood what happened, why his parents had left Slade behind, why another mouth to feed might have broken the budget. But the part of him that had always been connected to Slade didn't understand.

Still, he respected John Morgan and was thankful the man had taken him in. "The past is in the past."

John's brown eyes were troubled. "I wish that were

true. But every time you look at me I can see that it's not. Now that you're getting married yourself, maybe you'll see how things change when you do. Maybe you'll understand a man does the best with what he's got at the time.''

Hunter wasn't sure what John meant by that, but his life had become a round of working, traveling and women now and then whose names he forgot a week later. He was ready for a change.

It was almost eleven when Eve stepped inside the penthouse with Hunter. ''Are you going to bed now?'' she asked him as she followed him into the living room.

He stopped, turned and passed his gaze down her cream silk blouse and slacks. ''Do you have something else in mind?''

He was the only man who ever had the power to make her blush. ''I thought maybe we could talk.''

''We've been talking all evening.''

''We were making conversation with your parents. I like them a lot.''

''They seem to like you.''

''Is it my imagination or is something...awkward between you and them?''

Hunter frowned. ''Our relationship is complicated.''

''Your mother said that they'd christened you Hunter Coleburn Morgan but that you dropped the Morgan when you turned twenty-one. Why?''

''Because Coleburn is my real name.''

''But Hunter, they raised you....''

''Look, Eve, my relationship with them and Larry and Jolene has never been easy. If Mom and Dad had known they were pregnant, they would never have gone looking for a child to adopt.''

''They adopted you anyway.''

''Yes, they did. Because they felt obligated. I've always known that. Larry has always made sure that I've known that. He's their son, their *real* son.''

There was pain in Hunter's eyes, and Eve wished she knew the whole story and what had caused it. She was sure he wouldn't feel separated from his family unless there was a reason. ''I don't mean to pry.''

''Don't you?''

''I just want to know what makes you...you.''

He came over to her then and studied her. ''I suppose we have a lot to learn about each other.''

The electricity between them had been buzzing all night in a look, a glance, an inadvertent touch. In the car she'd been aware of his tall body, his heat, the strength in his arms as he'd driven his Lexus. At the Morgans', as they'd sat beside each other on the sofa after dinner, her heart had raced, and she'd had to make an effort to keep her mind on the conversation. Now in his blue eyes there was a silver light that she knew had something to do with that electricity.

''Hunter, this really isn't what I wanted to talk about.''

He slid his hand under the hair on her nape, and she trembled. ''Maybe we shouldn't talk at all,'' he murmured.

She knew what he had in mind, but another kiss could lead to the bedroom. First there was something she had to know.

''Hunter, are you involved with another woman?''

Chapter Three

Hunter's expression became unreadable. "Why do you ask?"

"I found something in the bedroom...a nightgown."

"I see. No, I'm not involved with anyone."

Hunter had seemed more open five years ago, more forthcoming. Had she done this to him? Or was she giving their brief interlude in his life too much importance? Still, before she went through with this marriage, she had to know something.

"On Tuesday, we're going to make promises. I need to know what that means to you."

His eyes became a deeper, darker blue, and she wondered what was going through his head. "I take marriage vows seriously, Eve."

She felt relieved, only it wasn't the complete assurance she was looking for. But how could she be sure of anything when they were entering a marriage of convenience? They needed time to get to know each other all over again. They needed time to figure out if feelings were left from the past and if they could build on them. If they *couldn't*...

She didn't want to think about that. Maybe a change of subject would help Hunter open up to her. "Tell me about the accident you were involved in."

A flash of surprise flickered in his eyes, then he said, "Why don't we get something to drink while we talk?"

As Eve went into the kitchen with Hunter, he opened the refrigerator door. "It's a little limited. I'm not here very much. Soda or orange juice?"

"Orange juice. Would you like me to stop at the store and pick up a few groceries?"

"Are you going to cook for us?" he asked with an arched brow.

"I can."

Removing the carton of juice, he studied her. "Didn't your housekeeper do all the cooking?"

"When Dad was away on business, I gave her time off. I can take care of myself, Hunter."

"You've changed," he commented as he took two glasses from the cupboard.

"I grew up."

Their gazes met and the air between them became charged again with memories, including her refusal to marry him five years ago.

She looked away first and took a seat at the small pine table. "Were your injuries from the accident serious?"

After he poured the juice, he came to sit across from her. "I don't remember much. One of my clients had a plane and his pilot flew me to Denver. I'd been in England for almost a month.''

"You spoke to Slade while you were there?''

"On Christmas Eve. I told him I'd call him as soon as I was back in the States. I intended to fly to Montana for a week or so.''

"Finding a twin out of the blue must have been a shock, but a wonderful Christmas gift, too. What was it like when you spoke to him for the first time?''

Hunter smiled. It was the smile she remembered...the one that had always weakened her knees.

"It was odd,'' he mused. "We were strangers and yet...'' He stopped. "There was this bond there, something we knew had always been there. We didn't say much that first time.''

"And then what happened?'' she prompted. She liked the warm look that always came into Hunter's eyes whenever he talked about Slade.

"It was snowing when we came in for a landing in Denver. I'd forgotten to fasten my seat belt. The next thing I knew we were careening out of control on the runway and I was thrown from my seat. I'm not sure if I felt the pain in my leg before I blacked out or not.''

"Your dad said you had a serious concussion.''

"I was unconscious for a few days. From what I understand, the doctors were afraid I wouldn't wake up again. When I did wake up... I'm not sure it happened all at once. I remember hearing Slade's voice. Something made me want to latch on to it. I heard him say I couldn't slip away now that we'd found each other. He told me to come back so he could get to know me. Somehow I pushed my eyes open, and there he was sitting by the side of my bed."

"He pulled you back," Eve murmured.

"Yes, he did." Hunter's voice went low and deep. "I'll always be grateful to him for that."

She sensed the emotion underlying Hunter's words. "Did Slade stay in Denver while you recuperated?"

"No, he couldn't. He was helping Emily run her ranch. She'd just had a baby. He'd hired on to help her with her chores and to search for me, and he ended up with a family. He's had a very different life than mine, but we've found we're not so different."

"It sounds as if you've gotten to know each other pretty well."

"We haven't spent a whole lot of time together. I went to Montana for his wedding and stayed about a week. We've only talked over the phone since then. But it's as if he's in the same room."

"It must be wonderful to have that kind of connection with a brother or sister. I always wished I had one. Now you have a sister and *two* brothers."

When Hunter finished his glass of juice, he stood, obviously not wanting to talk about the family he'd grown up with. "I have appointments all day tomorrow, but if you run into any snags with wedding plans, leave a message and I'll get back to you. I'm trying to clear my desk before we leave for Savannah."

"Besides the cake and flowers, your mother is going to help me shop for a wedding gown."

"I have a client who designs wedding gowns. I could contact her," he offered.

"Thanks, but I think I'd rather shop with your mother. I can get to know her better that way."

Eve stood, too, and placed her glass in the sink at the same time as Hunter. His gaze found hers, and he seemed to be looking for something. Her arm brushed his, skin against skin, heat against heat. Neither of them moved, and she held her breath.

When he leaned away, the contact was broken. "I'd like to go house hunting tomorrow night. I've sorted through the real estate information and there are about ten properties I'd like you to see."

"All in one night?" she asked with a smile.

"Unless we find the right one on the first try. Is there anything you particularly want or don't want in a house? Maybe I could eliminate a few."

"I don't have any expectations, Hunter."

"About the house or about the marriage?" he asked.

"I think both might be trial and error," she responded softly.

His blue gaze was intense, and she felt anticipation rather than expectation. Slowly he bent his head, as if he were giving both of them time to decide if they wanted to do this or not. She didn't move, afraid he wouldn't kiss her, afraid he'd decide this marriage wasn't a good idea after all. Maybe they needed another kiss as reassurance that they were making the right decision.

When his lips met hers, reassurance turned to desire. He didn't wait for her to part her lips but he pressed inside, taking her, making her sway toward him, needing to hold on for dear life.

But then he withdrew, and she looked up at him in need of more reassurance than before.

"Good night, Eve," he said, his voice husky. Then

he turned away from her and left the kitchen, leaving her to wonder if she'd ever understand this man she was going to marry.

"It's lovely, Eve."

Eve was standing on the dais in a large dressing room, looking in the mirror at her reflection. She examined the sweetheart neckline of the wedding gown, the short beaded white sleeves, the dropped waist, the full satin skirt. "I love it, but..."

"What's wrong?" Martha Morgan asked gently.

This morning they had chosen flowers, decided on a wedding cake and had lunch. Eve liked Martha and felt close to her already. This was the second bridal shop. The first one couldn't promise alterations by Monday. Now Eve answered her soon-to-be mother-in-law. "It's just that we're having a small wedding, and maybe I should buy something...simpler."

"A woman only gets married once, at least that's the way it's supposed to be."

Eve turned to face Martha. "I only intend to get married once."

The older woman smiled. "Well, then, dear, I think you should buy exactly what you want to buy and everyone else's opinion be hanged."

Eve laughed and turned to look at the gown again. It was exactly everything she wanted in a wedding dress. "All right, I will."

Next they picked out a veil. Eve chose a simple headdress beaded like the dress, with fingertip-length tulle. As the sales clerk left the dressing room to box it for her, Martha unbuttoned the tiny buttons on the back of the wedding gown.

"Thank you so much for helping me decide. It's times like this when I really miss..." She stopped for a moment, "I really miss my mother."

"How long has it been?" Martha asked gently as Eve stepped out of the dress.

"I was eleven when she died. Sometimes it seems like forever, other times it seems like yesterday."

"I know exactly what you mean." Martha carefully gathered up the wedding dress. "I lost my own mother a few years ago. We lived pretty far from each other, but I always knew she was there if I needed her." She paused and hung Eve's gown on its hanger. "I think Hunter has always felt the loss of his biological parents, too."

As Eve lifted her emerald coatdress with white piping from a hook and slipped one arm into it, she asked, "But you adopted him when he was very small, didn't you?"

"He was eight months old." Martha's face took on a pained expression. "But Hunter has always kept himself aloof from us. I've done reading on adopted children over the years, and some never feel part of the family who adopts them. But John and I are at fault, too. We tried for years to have children. When we didn't think we could have babies, we decided to adopt. We were so happy when the boys' home said they had twin boys who could be ours. Looking back..." She turned and hung Eve's gown on the hook. "We probably should have handled everything differently."

Slowly Eve buttoned her dress, hoping to learn more, but not wanting to be intrusive. "You adopted Hunter but not Slade."

"Yes. Several things happened at once. John was offered a job with the company in Montana. The salary wasn't any better but the chance for advancement was. About the time we were approved for the adoption, I found out I was pregnant, and then Hunter's twin became seriously ill and was hospitalized."

Martha sighed and shook her head. "With the move, a new baby on the way, the orphanage telling us it was better if we didn't adopt Slade until he was out of the woods, we had to make some decisions. The director at the boys' home was kind and assured us they'd find a family for Slade when he was well. We knew we were stretching our budget with two new mouths to feed and children to clothe, so we decided to take Hunter and start our new life in Montana. Ever since Hunter found out about Slade, he resents us for that."

"You never told him he had a twin?"

"No. Now I realize we should have. We should have explained our reasons for what we did very early. But within a year, Larry was born and then Jolene came along a year later. Our lives were full and we told ourselves we did the best thing for everyone concerned. And probably everything would have been all right if Larry had been a different type of child. Or if Hunter had been different, for that matter."

Eve wondered what Martha meant by that and waited to see if she'd explain.

Hunter's mother continued, "We weren't sure when we should tell Hunter he was adopted. Thirty-two years ago, adoption records were still kept sealed, and it wasn't spoken about as freely as it is now."

"How old was Hunter when you told him?" Eve asked.

"He was six. By that time, Larry was a handful, always wanting to be the center of attention, always wanting more than Hunter had. Jolene was the baby, requiring most of my care. When we told Hunter what adoption meant, that we had chosen him to be our son, he said in that mature way he has, 'But Larry and Jolene are your *real* children. I'm not, right?'"

Eve could imagine Hunter asking that, and she could only imagine what he felt when he did.

Smoothing over the folds of Eve's wedding gown absently, Martha said, "We tried to reassure him that he was indeed ours, too, but as Larry grew older, he seemed to always point out the differences to Hunter. Hunter had blue eyes, everyone else in the family had brown eyes. Larry let Jolene tag along with him and shut Hunter out. We always encouraged Larry to include Hunter, too, but that boy has a mind of his own."

Martha shook her head again. "And that's the way it's been ever since. I think Hunter saw things that weren't there. Larry was involved in athletics—mainly football and basketball. Those games were at night, so John and I tried to get to them. Hunter went out for track and the meets were after school. We couldn't attend most of them. Hunter won awards with the debate team, but Jolene had dance recitals by then."

She looked sad and troubled. "I don't know, Eve. Sometimes I look back on it and I think I wasn't a good mother to Hunter. John carries his share of the guilt, too. When Slade came searching for Hunter, it was as if everything Hunter had ever believed about us was reinforced. We had left his brother behind.''

Martha seemed to be unburdening herself by telling Eve. It sounded as if the Morgans had carried a lot of guilt over the years. ''But you did love Hunter...and you do now.''

''Oh, yes. We did and we do, and we're still hoping that sometime he'll realize that.''

After a moment, Eve said, ''Thank you for telling me.''

''Thank you for asking. It means you truly do care about our son.''

Eve *did* care about Hunter. Five years ago, for two weeks, she had dated him, talked with him, laughed with him, made love with him and had been afraid to decide her future based on a whirlwind of emotions she'd never known before. If she hadn't lost their baby...

She couldn't think about that now, and it might be better to wait until the wedding preparations and the wedding itself were over before she told Hunter about it. They needed time to get closer...time to begin building a future.

Hunter had rolled up his white shirtsleeves and looked as sexy as ever as they drove out of the city. He'd come into the apartment, shrugged off his suit coat and tugged off his tie, ready to begin house hunting.

When they'd left the city behind, he said, ''We're meeting Sheila at the house at seven-thirty.''

''Sheila?''

''The real estate agent. Did you eat?''

Eve had brought home two bags of food from a corner market. "Just some yogurt."

He grinned. "Yogurt?"

"I eat light." His glance was quick but thorough as it passed over her body, and she felt the thrill of knowing he found her attractive.

"I called Douglas Creighton this afternoon," Eve remarked.

"Who's he?"

"My father's lawyer. I told him we were getting married on Tuesday, and I wanted him to make sure the ownership of the paintings was transferred into your name."

"Once we're married, we'll both own them."

"I offered them to you, Hunter, and I meant it. This way if anything should happen..."

His voice was steady and deep. "You mean if the marriage shouldn't work out?"

She didn't want to allow for that possibility, but she had to. "They'll be yours, Hunter, no matter what."

He didn't respond, keeping his eyes on the road ahead of him.

An hour and a half later, they drove up in front of the fourth house on their list. It was dark now, but a floodlight had been placed on the lawn to illuminate the front. Hunter had been quiet and distant as they'd looked through the first three houses, only asking questions of the agent about the properties. He hadn't given any hints as to what he liked best, or if one had been to his liking more than another.

As they parked, this house caught Eve's eye more completely than the others had. Curves softened the accent lines over doors and windows. She could see it was brick and siding and had a multigabled roofline. The front door was topped by a half-round window.

"This one has character," she murmured.

He looked over at her in the shadows. "You didn't say much about the others."

"Neither did you. What did you think?"

"The yard was too small with the first one. I didn't like all the levels of the second one. And the third one didn't have anything to distinguish it from any other house. But this one..." He stopped.

Coming around to her side, he opened her door and offered her his hand. She took it. His fingers were warm, his hand large, and she liked the feel of it around hers. But when she stepped up onto the curb, he released her.

As soon as the agent opened the front door, Eve knew she liked the house. The barrel-vaulted entry led into a family room with a dramatically vaulted ceiling. There was a formal living room and dining room to the left. An open staircase divided the foyer from the family room, breakfast room and kitchen. The white brick fireplace with a raised hearth welcomed them into the family room, and there were beautiful drapes in blue-and-rose flowers in the living room, as well as pin-striped window dressing in rose and cream in the dining room. A short hall led to a suite behind the living room.

Hunter seemed to take a special interest in that before they went through the kitchen, with its work island and granite countertops, to a flagstone patio, double-car garage and laundry room. Upstairs, the master suite and bath were spacious. Two other bedrooms completed the tour.

The real estate agent's pager went off, and she said, "I'll take this outside. You wander around. Take as long as you like."

"What do you think?" Hunter asked as they walked back to the master suite.

"I like it very much," Eve said. "It looks new, yet the drapes and blinds already make it seem like a home."

"The family who owned it only lived here a year. They built it, and then the husband was transferred. It's reasonably priced because they don't want to carry a double mortgage."

"It really does seem perfect. Unless you think it's too big."

"Too big? Not at all. Not if we're going to start a family." The look he gave her said that had been the deal.

"I suppose children would fill it up quickly." The thought pleased her.

"We could put your father's art collection in that suite downstairs and have some work done so that it's climate controlled. I could use the sitting room adjacent to it for my office."

Looking around the master suite again and at the dormered window with its window seat, Eve imagined Hunter's huge bed here...the two of them sharing it. A thrill of excitement sizzled through her and when she turned to Hunter, he was watching her. "I really do like the house, Hunter. I think we could turn it into a home."

He came over to the center of the room then, where she was standing. "If we can settle on it quickly, we could move in when we get back from Savannah."

"Don't you have to get a loan approved, have a title search done?"

"I know someone who can speed up the title search. And I don't need a loan. After I sell the condo, we'll have a college fund for at least one child."

Again she thought of telling him about the miscarriage. But the time didn't seem right, not with them standing in the middle of an empty room, the real estate agent outside.

He was standing close to her, towering over her, and seemed to expect a response from her, some sign that she wanted the same things from their marriage that he did.

"Do you have a college picked out, too?" she teased.

"Harvard."

When he suppressed a grin, she laughed and shook her head. "I should have known."

As they gazed at each other, the attraction that had always been there between them seemed to vibrate in the empty house. A bit nervous with it, not sure how to act even though they were going to be married, Eve told him, "I bought my wedding gown today. I was concerned it was too...elaborate, but your mother didn't seem to think so. I know we're just having a small wedding—"

"You have excellent taste, Eve. I'm sure what you've chosen will be fine. I do have a tux," he said with a slight smile.

"I didn't know how formal you'd want it to be."

"We'll have to go to the courthouse tomorrow for the marriage certificate. I made arrangements for the honeymoon suite at the hotel. Is there anything we haven't covered?''

Her mind and world were spinning with the speed of how her life was changing. It was hard to believe that in less than a week she'd be married to this man who had invaded her dreams for five years. ''You've thought of everything.''

''Maybe we should seal our decision to take the house.''

''With a handshake?'' she asked, wanting his kiss, wanting the silver desire in his eyes.

''I think we can do better than a handshake.''

When his arms came around her, the new life they were going to embark on didn't seem quite as daunting. And when his lips came down on hers, she reached up to twine her arms around his neck. As Hunter kissed her, passion sparkled in a way she'd never known it. He'd been her first lover. Their passion had been so all-consuming that one night that he'd never guessed. A fall from a horse in her teens had claimed her clinical virginity. Nothing else had mattered that night except the two of them being as close as they could get. As before, his desire uncapped the well of passion that she'd protected all these years.

Eve's response to Hunter's kiss made him shudder. What was it about this woman? How could she make him need so desperately? Why did she make his sexual hunger come alive in a way he'd never experienced with anyone else? The kiss wasn't enough, and the thought of not going any further was dismissed with a recklessness he'd forgotten he'd possessed.

One hand slid to the base of her neck as he took the kiss deeper. His other slipped between them, going to the buttons on her dress. He remembered the look and feel and touch of Eve's body. He remembered how the sight of her had aroused him then and how the thought of it aroused him now. He undid the first shiny gold button easily and then the second and the third. Forays of his tongue were met with fervent ones by hers. The bra she wore fastened in the front, and quickly he unfastened it.

When her breath caught, he felt male satisfaction that he could take her breath away. She certainly took his. He let his hand lie between her breasts for a few moments, taunting them both, but then he captured her, pressed his palm against her, savoring the satin softness, the roundness. As he brushed his thumb over her nipple, she gasped, and he broke the kiss. The overhead light in the room was bright, and he leaned away slightly to look at her. Her cheeks were flushed, her lips were pink, her eyes were shining, sparkling with a passion he'd aroused. He scooped her into his arms and carried her over to the window seat, kneeling before her and bending his head to her nipple. When his tongue rasped over it, she moaned and he did it again.

"It's going to be good between us, Eve, so very good."

He wanted her to anticipate their wedding night. He wanted her to tremble with excitement when she thought about it. He wanted her to come to their marriage with as much need for him as he had for her. If he could tie her to him with passion, they might have a chance.

She only needed his name to claim her father's inheritance. He needed her body for the satisfaction he yearned for, for the child he dreamed of fathering. His need was greater than hers and he couldn't let her see that. All his life he'd learned that needing a family didn't make him part of one. He'd learned that seeking approval didn't mean earning it. He'd learned that giving could be met with rebuff and rivalry. Somehow he had to tie Eve to him, and if it took pleasure to do it, then that's what he'd use.

Molding his hands to both of her breasts, he circled them temptingly, teasing her and himself, bringing soft pants from her lips. He kissed each one of them with tiny, fluttering kisses that made her say his name. The sound of it on her lips was a husky temptation in itself. He took one nipple into his mouth, rimming it, toying with it, finally suckling it, and she cried out.

This is what they'd do in this room.

He felt his own hands shaking, and groaned. That's the power she had over him...the power he wanted over her. The best way to keep power was to wield it carefully.

At this moment Eve wanted him. He intended to keep her wanting him.

When he took his hands from her breasts, she protested. He held her head between his palms and kissed her thoroughly and deeply, letting it last until he thought he'd burst from his own needs.

But then he withdrew, dropped his hands and stood, looking down at her.

Eve's gaze was questioning and a bit lost. "Hunter?"

"I don't think we want to christen the bedroom quite yet. Sheila could walk back in here at any minute."

Eve looked mortified that she'd forgotten, and when she looked down at her open dress and bra, her cheeks blazed even brighter. "You're right, of course."

He noted with satisfaction that her fingers trembled when she fastened her bra. After she closed her dress, she stood looking uncertainly at him.

Trying to hide his desire for her, trying to appear unaffected by what had just happened, he asked, "So are we ready to clinch the deal on the house?"

Her fingers ran through her hair. "If it's what you want."

"It's what I want." Hunter realized he couldn't let Eve see just how badly he wanted *her*.

Because five years ago he'd shown her how desperately he'd needed her, and she'd walked away.

Chapter Four

The bubbles in the champagne tickled Eve's nose as she took a sip. This was the night before her wedding to Hunter. Martha had invited them to a prewedding celebration so that she could meet the rest of Hunter's family. So far the conversation had been limited to the heaviness of the traffic and the weather. Hunter's presence as he sat casually on the arm of her chair, handsomely dressed in a navy blazer, slacks and a white collarless shirt, was disturbing yet welcome, too, as she looked across the room at Larry Morgan and his wife, Midge. Hunter's sister, Jolene, sat beside Midge on the sofa. A few minutes ago John had excused himself, and Martha had gone to the kitchen to check on dinner.

Eve took another appraising look at Larry. He was good-looking in an average sort of way. His blond hair was slicked back with styling gel or hair spray, and his brown eyes were lighter than John's and Martha's.

He was wearing a black suit, double-breasted, with a gray-and-black tie. Midge had blond hair that, by the darkness of the roots, Eve could tell wasn't natural. She was almost as tall as her husband and gestured quite a bit when she talked.

In contrast, Jolene Morgan had her father's dark brown hair and her mother's wide-set, dark brown eyes. She was slender and delicate and smiled shyly at Eve often.

No one seemed to know exactly what to say.

"This wedding is awfully sudden, isn't it?" Larry asked anyone in general.

Hunter shrugged. "We couldn't find a good reason to wait."

Larry's eyes narrowed. "Just a couple of weeks ago you had a blonde on your arm in the newspaper. Were you in Georgia then, Eve?"

Eve herself had worried about that blonde too many times to count.

Over the weekend, she and Hunter had been busy with shopping for furniture for the house, generally making sure everything was set for the wedding tomorrow evening, as well as getting ready for the trip to Savannah. Hunter had spent time on and off at his office and, for the most part, they hadn't had much chance to be alone. Eve had felt embarrassed by her abandoned response to him Thursday evening in the house they were going to buy, and his casual attitude afterward. She knew he was a lot more experienced in sexual matters than she was, but she wished their kisses could rock him half as much as they rocked her.

"Yes. I was in Georgia then."

Hunter dropped his arm casually across her shoulders. "That photograph in the paper was taken after a business dinner. Barbara Kellogg is a client."

"I see." There was implied criticism in Larry's tone.

Jolene moved forward on the sofa. "Mom and Dad told me that you settle on a house tomorrow morning. Where's the property?"

After explaining the location, Hunter took a sip of his champagne.

"That's a wonderful area," Jolene said. "I understand the architect worked with the trees and the natural elements already there instead of tearing everything out."

Larry addressed Eve. "You'll be spending a lot of time there alone, I suppose. I was surprised Hunter found someone who could put up with his work hours and his traveling."

Straightening in her chair, Eve felt her temper spark. In spite of the opinion she'd started to form about Larry from Hunter and Martha, she'd nevertheless decided to meet him tonight with a clean slate. Yet his comments made it hard for her to remain objective. "It's all in your perspective," she said sweetly. "Hunter's hours will provide us with lots of opportunities for late-night dinners. And the traveling? Well, it will be a terrific opportunity for me to do some sight-seeing while he works, I imagine." Though Hunter had never said he'd take her with him.

"I'd like to see more than the outskirts of Denver," Midge complained. "But Larry's always too busy with work or softball."

Her husband frowned. "I promised you a trip to Europe later in the year."

"You did?"

"You mustn't have been listening," he said smoothly.

"If you're serious, I'll have to stop at the travel agent's and get all kinds of brochures. Then we can really plan where we are going. Hunter's been everywhere. I'm sure he can recommend the best places to see."

Before Hunter could comment, Larry offered, "If you're going to settle on the house tomorrow morning, that means you'll see each other before the wedding. Bad luck."

"We don't believe in superstitions," Hunter replied in a firm voice.

A beeping came from Hunter's pager. When he checked the number, he said, "It's Slade. I'll call from the kitchen."

"Your cell phone died?" Larry gibed.

"It's in the car. I didn't want business to interfere tonight unless it was absolutely necessary." With that, he stood and went to the kitchen.

"So...you're from the South," Midge said to Eve.

Larry picked up the conversational ball, such as it was. "Sweet Southern charm seems to be alive and well if Eve is any indication." He gave her a smile she supposed was intended to be ingratiating.

"Thank you, but I'm not sure Southern women are different from other women."

"Oh, they must be," Larry protested. "I don't know many women from around here who would want their husbands tending to some of the beauties Hunter has as clients."

Eve couldn't decide if Larry was nasty by nature or

had to work at it. "I suppose the trick is not seeing Hunter's clients as rivals. I'll be his wife, Larry. I'll be the woman he comes home to."

Larry looked taken aback, as if he hadn't expected such a forthright response.

"Eve," Hunter called from the kitchen. "Come here a minute, will you?"

Grateful for the interruption, Eve stood, and politely excused herself from the living room.

In the kitchen, Martha gave her a smile as Hunter handed her the phone. "It's Slade. He'd like to say hello to you."

Eve took the receiver. "Hello?"

"This is Slade Coleburn, Eve. I just wanted to tell you that Emily, Mark, Amanda and I are sorry we can't come to the wedding."

"I'm sorry, too. Hunter speaks very highly of you."

Slade chuckled. "Well, that's right nice of you to tell me that. We think highly of him. This wedding was pretty sudden."

"Yes, it was." She wondered if Hunter had told Slade the truth yet about their upcoming nuptials.

"We're planning to come to Colorado for a visit once you get back from Savannah and get comfortable in your new house. As long as we know ahead of time, we can take a week or so. That is, if a visit is all right with you. We don't want to barge in if you're trying to get your feet on the ground. We can stay in a motel."

"No, you won't stay in a motel," she protested quickly. "We'd like you to stay with us." She was eager to meet Hunter's twin. "We'll call you once we're back from Georgia."

"All right. We'll look forward to it. Now let me put Emily on the line. She wants to say hello, too."

Hunter watched Eve as she spoke with Slade and then with Emily. She was natural with them as if she'd been talking to them all her life. But then, Slade and Emily invited that kind of response.

When Eve hung up the phone a few minutes later, she smiled at Hunter. "They're nice people."

Martha picked up a platter of Cornish hens. "I've never met Emily, but Slade stayed here while Hunter was in the hospital." Martha glanced at Hunter. "He's a fine man and I wish..." Her words trailed off.

A look passed between Hunter and his adoptive mother and both their gazes were filled with pain. But neither said anything until Hunter crossed to Martha and took the platter from her hands. "I'll carry this in for you."

For the most part, dinner was pleasant. Seated next to Jolene, Eve asked questions about her work. Hunter's sister was animated when she spoke about it, as if she enjoyed it immensely. Larry took jabs at Hunter whenever he could, but they seemed to roll off Hunter's back. If this had been the pattern throughout Hunter's childhood, Larry's antagonism had to have affected him in some way.

After dessert, John Morgan stood and addressed Eve and Hunter. "We want you to know how happy we are about your wedding tomorrow. We considered what we could get you for a wedding present, and we came up with something a little different." He held up a small key. "This is for the two of you. In a few minutes I'll show you what it opens. Larry, do you want to come help me, please? We'll bring it into the living room."

Hunter accepted the key for the two of them and held it in his palm.

"Do you have any idea what it is?" Eve asked, leaning close to him.

When he turned to look at her, his lips could have easily brushed her temple, but he just shook his head. "I've no idea."

They waited in the living room, and a few minutes later Larry and John carried in a cedar chest.

"It's beautiful." Eve went to the chest and knelt in front of it. It was cherry wood with carvings of roses in the corners and under the lock. Behind her, she was aware of Larry moving over to stand beside Hunter, and she heard his low words.

"They offered it to me when I got married, but Midge wanted all new furniture, so Mom and Dad gave us money instead."

Eve glanced over her shoulder at Hunter. As a skilled lawyer and negotiator, he must be used to keeping his expression unreadable. It was unfathomable now.

John looked embarrassed by Larry's comment. "We thought the two of you would appreciate this. I know Hunter is a connoisseur of fine craftsmanship, and Eve told Martha about the furniture she cherishes that belonged to her mother. With your new house, we thought you might be able to find a place for it and eventually hand it down to your children as it was handed down to your mother. But if you'd like a different type of wedding present—"

"No," Hunter said quickly, running his hand over

the top of the chest. Then he looked up at his father. "We'll put it in our bedroom at the foot of the bed."

Eve heard the emotion in Hunter's voice but wasn't sure anyone else could. When he handed her the small key, she unlocked the chest and the smell of cedar wafted out. Looking inside, she saw a large envelope lying on the bottom of the chest. It had her name and Hunter's written on it.

Taking it out, she opened the envelope and read the wedding card. It brought tears to her eyes. She passed it to Hunter and he read it, too. "Thank you," she told the Morgans for both of them.

"You're most welcome," Martha said. "We can keep the chest here until you're ready for it. Just say the word."

As Hunter drove back to the penthouse that evening, he switched on the CD player and didn't talk. Eve wondered about the thoughts that might be going through his head. She certainly had a parade of them. She should be frozen with fear at all the changes to her life that were happening so fast, but she wasn't.

After they parked, rode the elevator to the penthouse and went inside, she decided to try to talk to Hunter about his family. "I think Larry's a very insecure man."

Hunter gave her a quick glance as he shrugged off his blazer. "I've never understood him and I never will."

Folding his jacket over his arm, he changed the topic. "We have a big day tomorrow. I guess we ought to turn in. If you do have a superstition about not seeing the groom before the wedding, you don't have to go along to the settlement tomorrow morning. I can take care of it myself."

She didn't believe in superstitions, but that wasn't what had gotten her attention. Hunter's tone had. "Don't you need me to sign something?"

"No. The paperwork will be in my name."

His announcement caught her off guard, but then the meaning sank in. "You mean the house will be yours."

"Yes."

Suddenly she remembered something Hunter had said. *Your inheritance is* your *money.* "Will we be keeping our finances separate?"

His gaze didn't leave hers. "I thought that would be best. As you said, if for some reason this doesn't work out, we'd have a tangled mess otherwise."

A tangled mess. Not work out.

Suddenly she saw something so clear in Hunter's gaze that she didn't know how she'd missed it before. He didn't trust her. He didn't trust that she'd go through with the wedding. He didn't trust that she'd stay if she did. And if he didn't trust her, she doubted if any of the feelings he once had for her remained.

Then why was he marrying her? Simply for the family he wanted? If he didn't trust her, how could a bond develop between them? Could a marriage built on desire and convenience last?

"Whatever you think is best," she murmured. "Maybe I will stay here tomorrow morning."

"I'm going into the office for a while before the settlement. I'll take my tux along and get ready there."

She wished Hunter would tell her what he was really thinking and feeling. She wished she knew what he really thought of her. "Then I guess I won't see you until I walk down the aisle."

Silent for a few moments, he finally said, "That's right. If you need me, just dial my pager number. What time would you like a limo to stop here to pick you up and take you to the church?"

Apparently he'd thought of everything. "Around five-thirty?" she asked. "I'll be getting dressed at the church. That should give me enough time."

"All right. I'll see you at the altar at seven."

He was gazing at her with that intense look of his, and she wished he'd come closer. She wished he'd take her in his arms. But he didn't.

Turning away from him, she murmured good-night and went down the hall to her room. Tears pricked in her eyes, but she blinked them away. This marriage had been her doing, and all she could do was hope the best would come of it.

As the organ processional played and Eve walked down the aisle of the church, she took Hunter's breath away. She was the most beautiful woman he'd ever laid eyes on. But he couldn't tell her that. He couldn't tell her a lot of things. Five years ago he'd opened himself up to her. He'd told her how beautiful she was. He'd told her what a difference she could make to his life.

And she'd pulled away. She'd retreated from him then, and she could leave again after they married. One day she could wake up and decide this sudden marriage was the last thing on earth she wanted. She could decide that Denver was the last place she wanted to live. She could decide that their marriage had been a mistake.

There was only one way she might stay. If she got pregnant, they could raise their child together and it would be a bond to make them both hold fast. In a sense, she was an orphan now and she needed someplace to belong. The sooner she became pregnant, the sooner he'd feel as if they had a chance.

The organ music swelled as Eve came forward. Hunter crossed to the center of the aisle, holding his arm out to her. She took it and they both faced the minister and the altar. As the last rays of daylight beamed through the stained glass windows, they listened to the minister, said their vows and exchanged gold wedding bands.

At the end of the ceremony when the minister said, "You may now kiss your bride," Hunter lifted her veil, took her in his arms and kissed Eve, intending to keep it light...short...sweet. But passion glanced through him like lightning. Eve responded as if it was the most important kiss of her life, and suddenly applause broke out among the guests.

Hunter lifted his head, and when she looked at him, he couldn't believe how desperately he wanted her. But he couldn't let her see that. His passion had scared her once before; so had his certainty in everything he'd wanted. They were going to take this slowly, and this time he'd be prepared if she said goodbye.

In the nave of the church, Hunter stopped with Eve and wanted to tell her how beautiful she looked. But instead, he said, "We forgot something."

"What?"

"A photographer. I never even gave it a thought."

She looked relieved. "Your mom and dad have a camera, and so does Jolene. They've been taking pictures. We'll have those."

Then the guests began entering the nave of the church, congratulating them.

The reception at the five-star hotel Hunter had chosen went without a hitch. Eve was gracious and friendly to Hunter's friends, and the evening passed quickly with glasses of champagne, an excellent meal, topped with wedding cake and ice cream. At the end of the evening, both John and Martha hugged Eve and Hunter and told them they'd see them when they returned from Savannah. Then Hunter escorted Eve to the elevator and it sped them to the honeymoon suite.

Hunter let Eve precede him through the door.

This morning, Eve had finished packing her bags for tonight and for their trip to Savannah. The limo driver had taken care of her luggage, telling her he'd make sure it was in the honeymoon suite for tonight. The closet door was open now and she saw her garment bag hanging beside Hunter's. As her gaze passed over the sitting area with its love seat, television, table and chairs, and up the two steps to the raised area where a king-size bed was covered in a red-and-gold spread, she saw her suitcase sitting beside Hunter's on the luggage rack.

Not sure what to do next, she watched Hunter as he slipped off the jacket to his tux and hung it in the closet, then uncinched his cummerbund. After he tossed the satin band over the arm of the chair, he came to stand before her. "We have an early flight tomorrow. We should probably turn in."

Turn in. Sleep with her husband. Come together in the union that was made for a wedding night.

"All right." When her fingers went to her veil to unfasten the combs, one stuck.

Hunter untangled it for her and placed the veil on the chair with his cummerbund. "Do you need help with your gown?" he asked, his voice husky.

Her reply would set the mood. Her reply would tell him whether or not she wanted him to make love to her. "Yes, I do. Can you unfasten the buttons in the back?"

The blue of his eyes was as deep as the ocean and just as mysterious.

She wished she could understand what she saw there. Was there more than desire?

"Turn around," he commanded.

After she did, she felt his fingers first on the top button and then the next. His skin was fire as it brushed hers, leaving a scalding heat. She trembled. She felt him undo a third button and a fourth. But then he stepped closer and when his lips brushed the back of her neck, her breath caught. He kissed her nape again and she couldn't wait for more of his kisses, for his hands to touch her skin more thoroughly.

When he finished unbuttoning the dress, she let it fall from her arms and pushed it down with her slip. The garments formed a satin puddle on the floor. She turned to Hunter and he gathered her to him, sealing his lips to hers, kissing her with a ferocity she hadn't expected. Then he scooped her into his arms and carried her to the bed.

He laid her down, then his fingers went to the studs on his shirt. She sat up and helped him, as eager for him to be rid of his clothes as he was. Her hands brushed his chest and he sucked in a breath. Their gazes met. She thought she saw need there, and she hoped it was more than physical.

The studs gone, Hunter made quick work of his shirt and trousers and then his briefs. She'd taken off her shoes and panty hose but was still wearing a white lace bra and the filmiest of panties.

Hunter sat down beside her and stroked her hair behind her ear. "You're beautiful."

Her gaze passed over his well-muscled body and his arousal. "You are, too."

She wanted him to know she wasn't afraid, that she could be his equal this time by expressing her passion without hesitation, without doubts. She wasn't any more experienced than their first time—she'd never been with a man other than Hunter—but she didn't know if he was ready to hear that, any more than she was ready to say it. The wrong word, the wrong move could tip the delicate alliance they'd formed.

"I don't want to rush you, Eve. If you're not ready for this—"

"I want to be a real wife, Hunter. I'm ready."

When he bent to her, he kissed her again with a possessiveness that created a fierce yearning inside her. She passed her hands down his back, marveling at his physical prowess, appreciating the feel of him in her arms. She remembered this. She'd longed for it so often in her dreams...and she suddenly knew why. She didn't just still have feelings for Hunter Coleburn.

She still loved him.

The realization was glaringly bright, glaringly terrifying. What if he had no feelings for her? What if he decided he couldn't forgive her doubts of five years ago? What if he always kept himself removed?

But he wasn't removed now. His tongue told her he desired her.

Breaking the kiss, he looked down at her again and reached for the fastening on her bra and unclasped it. Then his gaze left hers, drifting to her breasts...her waist. He hooked his thumbs in her panties and pulled them off. Raining kisses on her throat and the skin above her breasts, he stroked her thighs until she parted her legs. She moaned when he touched her. Soft sighs escaped her lips as he flicked his tongue over one of her nipples and passed his hand between her legs again. When he came down beside her, she touched his chest and slid her hand down his stomach.

He groaned and then said, "Eve, I can't take much of that if you want to prolong this."

"We don't have to prolong it," she responded almost shyly.

His gaze held hers. "I want to make this pleasurable for you."

"It will be." She wished she felt free to touch him more intimately.

"What are you thinking?" he asked.

"That I want to please you."

He rose above her then. "You are pleasing me, Eve. I want you."

"I want you, too," she whispered.

The desire in his eyes became more mesmerizing. She couldn't take her gaze from his, not as he caressed her breasts until she moaned, not as he passed his hand down her stomach and touched the center of her desire.

"You *are* ready," he rasped.

With a slow, smooth thrust, he entered her.

They were one, and as he sank deeper and withdrew, then sank in again, she caught his rhythm and moved with him. "Oh, Hunter," she gasped. "You feel so wonderful."

Holding on to him tightly, she started the steep ascent to a wondrous mountaintop she'd climbed only once before. She reached the top quickly and teetered on the edge, raking her nails down Hunter's back. When she arched up against him, their movements seemed to explode into ripple after ripple of intense pleasure. His mouth came down on hers as she wrapped her legs around him, seeking to prolong everything, wanting to give Hunter such deep satisfaction he'd never want to separate from her. His thrusts were hard and she contracted around him, even as the giant erotic wave swept over her. Tearing his mouth from hers, he drove into her again, saying her name with such soul-stirring depth, tears came to her eyes. His life force surged into her, and she held him as he shuddered again and again.

Could she give her heart to him knowing she might lose it? Knowing he might break it? Knowing he wanted a family maybe more than he wanted her?

What would he say when she told him that they'd lost a child already?

Tomorrow would be soon enough to find the answers.

Tonight, she just wanted to hold on to him and believe that he wanted to hold on to her.

Chapter Five

Ida Clark, the housekeeper who had taken care of Emory Ruskin's domestic concerns for the past ten years, opened the door to Eve's childhood home before she could use her key. Gathering Eve into a tight hug, she finally pushed away to look at her. "Did you really get married while you were gone?"

Eve had called Ida to tell her of her marriage and to prepare her for the fact that they'd be packing up the house when she and Hunter came to Savannah. "Yes, I did." She stepped back next to Hunter. "Do you remember Mr. Coleburn?"

"Sure do," Ida drawled. "He likes his eggs over-easy and his coffee black."

Hunter laughed and extended his hand to her. "You have a good memory."

"That's my job," Ida returned. Then as she looked at Eve, she amended, "At least that *was* my job. The Garrisons said I can start with them whenever you're finished here."

"Will you be happy with them?" Eve asked, concerned.

"I'm sure I will. They're a nice couple. They have loads of grandchildren who visit them often, so that will keep me busy. But I..." She hesitated. "I'm going to miss you, as well as your father."

Eve's throat tightened and she fought back tears. "I'll miss you, too." Composing herself, she said, "We're going to put our things up in my room. I'm expecting Douglas Creighton for dinner this evening."

Ida nodded. "Mr. Creighton phoned this morning and said he'd be here at eight." As they moved across the foyer, the housekeeper said, "When you're ready to start packing just say the word. Joe's home from college and he can help us."

Joe was Ida's son and had often done odd jobs for Eve's father. "Thank you, Ida. Hunter and I will probably decide what furniture we want to have shipped to Denver, but I'll wait till morning to start packing up."

A few minutes later, Eve and Hunter climbed the wide staircase to the second floor. Eve wished she could feel some of the closeness to Hunter that she'd felt last night. For those few moments when they'd made love so passionately, it had seemed as if their hearts and souls had touched. When the alarm had gone off this morning and she'd awakened tucked close to Hunter's side, she'd hoped the closeness would spill over into the rest of their marriage. But after a kiss that Eve knew could have developed into a lot more, Hunter had broken away, slid out of bed and taken a shower.

She wished she knew what he was thinking. She

wished she knew if last night had affected him as much as it had affected her. But he was guarding himself too carefully for her to see or sense anything.

Her climb up the staircase reminded her of all those times as a child she'd run up or down, happy or sad, with friends or alone, on her way to bed, or eager to face a new day. She'd spent her entire life under the roof of this twelve-room house, and she was going to miss it dearly. It wasn't just the house itself, of course. There were so many memories attached to every piece of furniture, every rug, every smell, every picture hanging on the walls. Houses took on personas of their own and this one had always wrapped its arms around her, just as Ida had.

When they entered Eve's room, Hunter's gaze passed over the white canopy bed with its cover of blue-and-white stripes, pink roses and eyelet, as well as the rose carpeting, the pale blue velvet chaise and the bookshelves with their well-read volumes and childhood mementos.

He said, "It's just as I remembered it."

This is where they'd made love the first time. Her father had had an evening appointment and Ida had had the night off. She and Hunter had planned to go out to dinner and the theater. But in the house alone, their desire had gotten the best of them both.

After Hunter set down their two suitcases, he went to the doorway. "I'll get the garment bags. They're still on the porch."

Eve followed him to the top of the stairway and then, instead of going back to her own room, she crossed to the end of the hall and opened the door into her father's.

Nothing had been touched since the day Emory Ruskin had died. She hadn't been able to make herself put his robe in the closet or move his black wing-tipped shoes from the side of the bed. But now she knew she'd have no choice. Before she realized it, she was seated in his burgundy-leather wing chair, lifting his robe to her nose. It smelled like him and his aftershave. He'd worn that robe when he'd read her stories. He'd worn that robe on Christmas Eve when he'd watched her set out cookies and milk for Santa. He'd worn that robe after her mother died when he'd held her and they'd both cried.

She didn't realize she was crying now until Hunter came into the room, knelt down before her and took her hands in his. "I know you miss him."

She just nodded, her tears falling fast.

Standing, Hunter pulled her up into his arms, holding her tight, pressing his lips against her temple. She couldn't hold the sobs back and Hunter absorbed them, stroking her hair, making soothing circles on her back.

"It's okay," he murmured. "It'll be okay."

She hoped it would be. She hoped the missing would become less. She hoped in some way her dad was still with her. But right now the grief seemed to be all there was.

Finally Hunter led her to the bed and sat beside her. "Tell me what you remember most about your dad."

So many memories came rushing in that it was hard for her to choose. "I remember his pipe and the smell of cherry tobacco. I remember him sitting in his office, poring over the details of every business deal. I remember his favorite navy pin-striped suit. He always said it was his lucky suit and he always wore it when he had a business meeting with someone new. I remember how much he liked cherries jubilee and rare steak and sitting at the creek behind the house just watching the water flow over the rocks. He and Mom used to do that a lot when she was alive.'' Eve lifted her gaze to Hunter's. ''I'm afraid I'm going to forget the details...all the little things, and the big ones, too.''

''You won't forget. Not if you have reminders and pictures of things that hold special memories.''

''I want to believe that's true.''

They sat there together in silence for a little while.

Eventually Eve said, ''I remember how strong he was, how protective, and how I liked it but fought against it, too.''

After another silence, Hunter shifted on the bed and his knee brushed against hers. ''Why didn't you marry the man your father had picked out for you?''

In her heart, Eve knew they couldn't build this marriage on anything but truth. It was time to tell him about her pregnancy. Taking a tissue from the pocket of her slacks, she blew her nose to give herself a few moments to think, and then she stuffed the tissue back in her pocket. ''I've been wanting to tell you something, but the time just didn't seem right.'' She looked down at her hands in her lap and then she faced him. ''Six weeks after you left Savannah, I found out I was pregnant.''

Hunter looked stunned. ''With whose child?''

''It was your child. I'd never been with a man before you.'' She hurried on before his mind rushed ahead. "But then a couple of weeks later, I had a miscarriage."

He not only looked shocked, but disbelieving, and then his blue eyes became cold and his voice terse. "You weren't a virgin. There was no barrier."

"I guess clinically I wasn't a virgin. I'd fallen off a horse when I was fourteen and..." She shrugged, and she felt heat in her cheeks.

Hunter stood and walked over to the window. He stared outside as if he was searching for answers or maybe trying to control his emotions. But when he came back to her, his expression was as stern as before. "Why didn't you tell me about the pregnancy? If you had, maybe you wouldn't have miscarried."

She hadn't expected this vehement reaction from Hunter. To combat his accusation, she said, "I *did* try to contact you. But you were already involved with someone else."

"You're lying. I wasn't involved with anyone else, not for months after I left Savannah."

Maybe he didn't want to admit he'd taken another woman into his bed so soon after her, but he had. "I called your hotel room in Florence and a woman answered. It was late evening and I knew..." She stopped, drew her shoulders back and pulled herself together. Her pride kept her from giving him any further explanations, from pleading with him to believe her.

There was a look of betrayal in his eyes and so many doubts that she didn't know *what* to say. She suspected there was one thought eating at him. "I might have been confused after you left, Hunter, but I wanted the baby."

His gaze raked over her face, searching for the truth. Tension vibrated around them until he asked, "Can you have more children, or did you marry me under false pretenses?"

False pretenses? Did he think she would deceive him to get her inheritance? Apparently so. She'd been right when she'd guessed he didn't trust her. She wondered if he trusted anyone. All he wanted from this marriage was a baby. If that hadn't been obvious before, it certainly was now.

Icily, she answered him. "I had a thorough checkup before I came to Denver, and there's nothing to prevent me from becoming pregnant again."

"And that can be confirmed?"

"Yes," she answered, suddenly weary. "That can be confirmed. You can call Dr. Roberts if you want."

Hunter raked his hand through his hair and looked at her as if she were a stranger. "I deserved to know about this when it happened. You should have told me before the wedding ceremony."

What would have happened five years ago if she had tried to contact him after the miscarriage? Would her doubts about leaving home have vanished? Would she have realized she could follow him anywhere and be happy? She'd never know. But he was right that she should have told him before the wedding ceremony, because now, whatever she said would be suspect. She was going to have to earn his trust from ground zero.

"I'm sorry, Hunter. I should have told you before the wedding, but everything happened so fast...."

"That's no excuse, Eve."

No, it wasn't. She'd wanted to wait until she was

feeling closer to him, and now she didn't know if she'd ever feel close to him again. If he'd let her get close.

He went to the doorway. "I'm going to change and go for a jog. I'll be back in time to get showered before dinner."

Then he was gone, and she felt as if she'd lost him all over again.

As they sipped their after-dinner coffee, Douglas Creighton turned to Eve. "You've met the conditions of your father's will."

They'd made polite conversation throughout dinner, Hunter and Douglas discussing noteworthy legal cases that had been in the news recently. Hunter had barely looked at Eve, and she didn't know what to do. Where he'd been cautious before, now there was a protective wall between them that she couldn't begin to scale. But Douglas acted as if he hadn't noticed anything was amiss.

"Does that mean we can move some of the furnishings from here to Denver?" she asked.

"Oh, yes. The photocopy of your marriage license will be sufficient for my files. And I'm sure you want to get moved into that new house as soon as you can. We'll miss you here in Savannah, though. You know that, don't you, Eve?"

"Thank you for saying that. And I'll miss everyone in Savannah."

"If you hold on to the house, you could come back here for extended visits."

"It just doesn't seem practical, Douglas."

"Sometimes practical isn't always the best solution," he said sagely.

The conversation turned to real estate in Denver compared to real estate in Savannah, and then after a while Douglas looked at his watch. "Oh, my. It's almost ten o'clock. I should be going. After all, this is your honeymoon," he said with a knowing grin.

Eve glanced at Hunter, but he was taking a final swallow of coffee.

A few minutes later she walked Douglas to the door.

Before he opened it, he turned to her. "I wasn't a bit surprised when you called me to tell me you were marrying Hunter Coleburn. That's what your father had hoped."

"He expected it?"

"Yes, and I imagine now maybe you can see why your father wrote his will as he did."

With blinding insight she suddenly realized what her father had seen. She'd fallen in love with Hunter almost immediately and had glowed with the wondrous sensation. They'd gone out and taken long walks together, but at the end of Hunter's first week in Savannah, her father had warned her not to become infatuated, not to take the chance on a fledgling lawyer who didn't know if he could make a name for himself. He'd told her for the umpteenth time that she needed to marry into the society she knew, and give him grandchildren who would have a proud heritage as well as secure futures. Blunt as always, he'd told her Jerry Livingston was her future, not Hunter Coleburn.

She'd left her father's study that night more confused than she'd ever been. As she'd spent time with Hunter the next week, she'd realized her father had meant her to entertain him, not fall in love with him. There was no doubt that Emory Ruskin had expected her to obey him as she always had and follow his advice.

But maybe after her miscarriage, he'd realized how wrong he'd been. Or maybe that certainty had come years later when she was working and sleeping and not doing much else. Whenever it had been, he'd apparently seen this clause in his will as a way to see her happy.

Her heart swelled with love for her father, and then she hugged Douglas and saw him on his way.

When she went back to the dining room, Hunter was nowhere in sight.

Ida was removing the linens from the table. "Mr. Coleburn said he was going to take a walk. I think he went out the back."

Eve wanted to go after him, but she wasn't sure what she could say or do to make him trust her. Had there really been no other women in his life after he left Savannah? Had she made some kind of mistake? She didn't know. What she did know was that Hunter thought she was lying about trying to contact him.

She'd made a mess of things. Now somehow she had to figure out a way to convince Hunter to believe in her again, a way to make their marriage succeed.

Sweat dripped from Hunter's brow as a walk turned into another jog along the residential streets of Savannah. His chest tightened, not from the exertion of running, but from the thought of losing a child. He'd almost been a father. Almost.

He'd felt as if he'd been poleaxed after his conversation with Eve. She'd been a virgin when he'd taken her. He'd thought her shyness was simply inexperience. He'd never expected...

She'd been almost engaged to Jerry Livingston.

But it made sense in a way—her father keeping her protected as long as he could and Eve being afraid to venture into a relationship with a man. She had no reason to lie to him about her virginity, did she?

But she had to be lying about trying to contact him. He hadn't gone near another woman for months after he left Savannah. Maybe she was just trying to make herself look better. Maybe she thought he was gullible enough to believe her.

The Ruskin home came into sight again, and Hunter slowed to a walk.

A pregnancy. A child. A miscarriage.

Had she really wanted his child? Wouldn't an unwed mother in Eve's position pray for a miscarriage...or hope that something went wrong so she could go back to the life she'd intended to have?

He shook his head trying to make some sense out of the jumble of thoughts and questions. One thing he did know. He couldn't share that bed with her tonight. He wanted her in an elemental way that absolutely disconcerted him, but he couldn't make love to her tonight.

Not until he sorted some of this out.

When Eve awakened the following morning, she realized Hunter had never come to bed. She'd waited up till three, then tossed and turned most of the night, finally falling into a fitful sleep. Hurrying to the closet, she saw that his clothes were still there. At least he hadn't left.

Quickly she showered and dressed in red shorts, a white top and sandals, then went downstairs in search of her husband. She found him on the screened-in porch, holding a mug of coffee. He was looking out over the gardens in the backyard to the magnolias beyond.

She didn't know what to say to him, but they had to discuss yesterday. "You didn't come to bed last night."

He gave her a quick glance and stared out into the yard again. "I slept in one of the guest bedrooms."

Moving closer to him, she lightly laid her hand on his arm. "I'm sorry, Hunter. I don't know what else to say."

He faced her then. "There isn't anything you *can* say. You got pregnant and you didn't tell me. You miscarried and you didn't tell me."

"After it happened...there didn't seem to be any point," she murmured.

"I lost a child, Eve. I deserved to know that."

She could see the pain in his eyes and hear it in his voice, and she felt as if her heart were tearing in two. "I'm sorry," she said again. "I don't have an excuse except that I was confused, and I truly did think you had gone on with your life and it wouldn't matter."

"Then you didn't know me very well."

"How could I know you? We only spent two weeks together."

He drove his hand through his hair, walked over to the small glass table by the wicker settee and put his mug on it.

The distance between them was too great to ignore. If she didn't lessen it now, their marriage might be over before it began. "Hunter, I know this is between us now. Look, can't we get around it? Can't we make our marriage work?"

It was a while before he answered. "You've lived with this for five years. I just found out about it yesterday."

She approached him again, hoping he wouldn't turn her away. "I lost a child, too, Hunter. And even though it happened five years ago, every day I remember it. Every day I wonder what that child would have been like if he or she had lived."

When Hunter lowered himself to the settee, Eve sat beside him. "Are you going to fly back to Denver?"

"I told you I'd help you pack up the house. That's what I'm going to do."

"Are you going to sleep in the guest room again tonight?" she asked, because she had to know.

With the nerve working in his jaw, he shifted toward her. "Do you want to have a family with me?"

A family. Having one meant everything to him. She wanted so much more than a family, but she answered, "Yes. And I'll do whatever I have to so that we can get past this."

"Your father didn't say how long you had to *stay* married."

She could hear the suspicion and the underlying assumption that only her inheritance mattered to her. She had to convince him otherwise. "I think he knew that if I chose someone to marry, I would make every effort to make the marriage succeed."

Hunter's gaze probed hers and then studied her so

intently, she felt turned inside out. Finally he said, "Let's get some breakfast. We'll let the rest of the day take care of itself."

He was still angry with her. He was still trying to absorb a loss, and she had to give him a chance to work through it. She just hoped that when he did, they could start over again.

The day passed swiftly as Eve and Hunter decided what furniture to have moved to Denver and packed up those things Eve wanted to move with it. In the afternoon, they met with the real estate agent. Later in the midst of their packing, Hunter made arrangements with Ida for her son to drive Eve's car to Denver and then fly back home. He and Eve didn't talk much all day, and during dinner they simply discussed which movers would be the best to use and when the furniture should arrive.

After dinner, Eve wrapped her mother's good china while Hunter packed up Emory Ruskin's books. It was almost eleven when he came into the dining room and found her sealing a box.

"Are you ready for bed?"

She was hoping his question meant they'd be sleeping together tonight. "Yes."

Hunter took the box from the mahogany table and stacked it against the wall with the others. Then Eve turned off the light, and they walked together to the stairs.

Following her to her room, Hunter didn't say a word as they went inside. She felt awkward, not sure of what to say or do. Hunter used the bathroom, and when he came out he caught her standing naked by the bed, her gown on the spread.

"You might as well leave it off," he said as he turned back the covers.

She could feel herself blushing. Switching off the light, she slid into bed beside him.

They lay there for a few minutes, the gulf between their naked bodies seeming like the width of the Grand Canyon. Moonlight shone softly through partially closed blinds, and Eve could see Hunter's profile. His jaw was tense, his arms by his sides. But he was aroused. She uncertainly laid her hand on top of his. When he shifted, she thought he was going to pull away, but he turned toward her and slipped his hand under her hair.

There was a mastery about Hunter, a sureness that told her he always knew exactly what he was doing. When his mouth found hers, she didn't know what to expect. The kiss was restrained at first. But when she touched her tongue against his lips, he groaned, held her tighter, then took the kiss deeper, and possessively demanded a wanton response.

As his restraint broke, Hunter mentally swore. He couldn't help kissing Eve as if he'd missed her all day. Because he had. He'd needed her, and he didn't want to need her. He didn't want to need anybody. Alone in the guest room bed last night, he'd cursed his body for wanting her.

He didn't know why she had the power to turn him inside out. He'd walked away from other women. He'd said goodbye easily and gotten on with his life. He'd taken pleasure and given pleasure and found basic satisfaction in that.

But with Eve...

The yearning and needing was so deep, he resented

her for it. She'd married him for her inheritance, and now she wanted to make the marriage work out of a sense of duty and maybe even responsibility to her father.

A small voice whispered, *She could still leave.*

He was used to being alone, so why was the idea of her walking away so wrenching?

She wouldn't say goodbye, not this time. He'd tie her to him with chains of desire and with children.

Rolling her onto her back, he let his body cover hers, chest to breast, hips to hips, need to need. "Am I too heavy?" he growled.

"No. I want you, Hunter."

Was she telling the truth? Did she want him nearly as much as he wanted her? It wasn't possible. Rising on his elbows, he kissed her face, and her neck, and her breasts until she was writhing restlessly under him. When he kissed her navel, her fingers delved into his hair. He kissed down farther and farther until she almost sat up.

"Hunter..."

"Shh. I'm going to kiss you everywhere."

And he did, until her hands clutched at his shoulders, until a sweet cry broke from her lips. Then he buried himself inside her. When he started moving, he could feel her pleasure coiling and breaking again. She cried his name, and he kissed her with a ferocious passion that screamed for release.

Minutes later he found it with a soul-shattering intensity that made him wish he could control his need, made him wish he could hold back his desire. He hated feeling vulnerable, and he felt that way when he joined with her. But he knew how to guard himself and he knew how to hide vulnerability. While he was doing that, he'd pray that Eve conceived his child.

MacMillan's Garden Center, on the outskirts of Birch Creek, had a wonderful reputation. Eve parked on the gravel outside the white gates that opened into the nursery.

She and Hunter had moved into the house two weeks after they'd gotten back from Savannah. Although new furniture had been delivered and everything they'd shipped from Savannah had arrived, she was still decorating and finding special pieces one by one.

Last week she'd been shopping in downtown Denver and had stopped at an art gallery. The conversation had turned into a part-time job and Eve was happy about that. Hunter often worked long hours. Decorating the house was fun, but she'd soon be finished. Working at the gallery would give her something fulfilling to do.

They'd been married for six weeks now, and she and Hunter had settled into a routine. But he was still distant. She couldn't seem to break through the barriers he'd erected around himself. The only time she really felt one with him was when they made love. He was a wonderful lover, giving her so much pleasure she felt she could die from it. But she wanted so much more than pleasure from him. Still praying their marriage could be more than a convenient way of life, she was going to show him she loved him every day— with every word, with every touch, with everything she did—and maybe eventually he'd realize he could trust her.

Maybe someday soon she could tell him how much she loved him...had always loved him.

The sun shone brightly on the greenhouses and the path of crushed marble leading into the nursery. There were a few customers here and there, pointing, looking, wandering up and down the rows of flowers, bushes and trees. Eve found her way to the perennials and the flats of geraniums. The pink ones caught her eye.

"Can I help you?"

Eve turned to find a pretty woman with honey-blond hair tied back in a ponytail, dressed in jeans and a T-shirt, with gardening gloves stuffed into her pocket. Eve suspected she was in her late twenties.

Smiling, she answered, "I hope so. My husband bought a house...." She stopped. "We bought a house and my husband said I can do anything I'd like with the gardens. I want to add a few bushes and flowers that will bring color at different times of the year."

The young woman extended her hand. "I'm Lauren MacMillan. And I'm sure that I or other members of my family can help you with whatever you want to do. Why don't you tell me exactly what you have in mind."

Eve took a piece of paper from her purse. "I'm not an artist, but this will give you an idea of what we have and what I want to do."

"You have an eye for layout," Lauren said. "Did you have training in design?"

"I have a degree in art history."

"You have an eye for color and detail, too. I've also noticed you have a beautiful Southern accent. Have you been here long?"

"Just since my marriage about six weeks ago."

"Congratulations," Lauren said. Her sparkling brown eyes were sincere.

"I'm still finding my way around," Eve admitted, "But one of our neighbors recommended your nursery. Mr. Olsen."

"Oh, yes, we did all of his landscaping. I drew up the plans myself."

Eve glanced at the drawing. "Besides what I've outlined here, I'd like to create a rock garden out back with a fountain in the middle, but I'm not sure where to start."

"Probably the best thing for me to do would be to take a look at your property. We could set up an appointment for next week if you'd like."

"That would be great." Eve thought about her work schedule.

"How about Monday afternoon about three?" Lauren asked. "That's usually a slow time around here, and I can get away easily."

"That's fine. I only work till noon on Monday."

"Where do you work?"

"At the Sandstone Gallery."

"Oh, I've been in there several times. They have beautiful paintings and sculptures." Lauren studied Eve's drawing again, then waved toward the greenhouses and the tables filled with flowers. "Why don't we take a tour of the nursery, and I'll show you what you have to choose from. Then when I come out on Monday, you might have an idea of what you want where."

It was a plan, and Eve felt her life needed some planning. Just as she had in decorating the house, she would put all her effort and love into planning their gardens. Then maybe Hunter would realize they were building a good life together. Maybe he'd let his guard down and let her love him.

Chapter Six

When Hunter came home from a quick trip to his
office Saturday morning to pick up some papers he
had forgotten, the smell of cinnamon surrounded him.
The end of May had turned hot. He'd dressed in shorts
this morning, intending to work in the yard when he
got back. He really should fly to Los Angeles soon,
but he'd put the trip on hold for the time being. Maybe
he'd talk to Eve and see how she felt about spending
a week in L.A. It was new to him…this discussing his
plans with someone.

Over the past few weeks, he'd learned Eve preferred
fresh air to air-conditioning, so he wasn't surprised to
find a breeze blowing the sheers away from the windows in the living room.

She'd done a magnificent job of decorating and
homemaking. He just wished…

What? That she'd get pregnant quickly?

Maybe that was it. Once she conceived, he'd feel

Here's a **HOT** offer for you!

Get set for a sizzling summer read...

with **2 FREE ROMANCE BOOKS** and a **FREE MYSTERY GIFT!**

NO CATCH! NO OBLIGATION TO BUY!

Simply complete and return this card and you'll get **2 FREE BOOKS** and **A FREE GIFT** – yours to keep!

Visit us online at www.eHarlequin.com

- The first shipment is yours to keep, **absolutely free!**

- Enjoy the convenience of Silhouette Romance® books delivered right to your door, before they're available in stores!

- Take advantage of special low pricing for **Reader Service Members** only!

- After receiving your free books we hope you'll want to remain a subscriber. But the choice is always yours—to continue or cancel, any time at all! So why not take us up on this fabulous invitation, with no risk of any kind. You'll be glad you did!

315 SDL C26P

215 SDL C26K
(S-R-OS-06/00)

▼ DETACH HERE AND MAIL CARD TODAY! ▼

Name:	
	(Please Print)
Address:	Apt.#:
City:	
State/Prov.:	Zip/ Postal Code:

The Silhouette Reader Service™ —Here's how it works:

Accepting your 2 free books and gift places you under no obligation to buy anything. You may keep the books and gift and return the shipping statement marked "cancel." If you do not cancel, about a month later we'll send you 6 additional novels and bill you just $2.90 each in the U.S., or $3.25 each in Canada, plus 25¢ delivery per book and applicable taxes if any.* That's the complete price and — compared to cover prices of $3.50 each in the U.S. and $3.99 each in Canada — it's quite a bargain! You may cancel at any time, but if you choose to continue, every month we'll send you 6 more books, which you may either purchase at the discount price or return to us and cancel your subscription.

*Terms and prices subject to change without notice. Sales tax applicable in N.Y. Canadian residents will be charged applicable provincial taxes and GST.

their marriage would be more solid. He'd called her doctor before they'd left Savannah, and the man had assured Hunter that Eve was perfectly healthy and capable of having children. So she hadn't deceived him to secure her inheritance.

Walking into the kitchen, Hunter found his wife on her hands and knees, wiping up something on the floor. She was so beautiful with her cheeks flushed and loose tendrils of hair around her face that had escaped her ponytail. Dressed in pale pink knit shorts with a spaghetti-strap top, she caused his hormones to go into overdrive.

Soapsuds tumbled out of the bucket onto the floor and he couldn't help smiling at the picture she made there. He still thought of her as a debutante.

She looked up. "I spilled the pitcher of iced tea. What a mess."

He crouched down at the bucket. "Did the pitcher break? Should you be watching out for glass?"

"No, it was a plastic one. Just a mess. Tea, ice cubes, lemon." She sat back on her haunches.

His smile returned when he saw the soapsuds on her arm. "I didn't know you knew how to wash up a floor."

She took a handful of soapsuds from the bucket and blew them at him. "There's a lot of things I know how to do that you don't know anything about."

The suds landed on his nose. He scooped a handful from the bucket and blew them back at her.

This time she retaliated by ducking her hand in the bucket and flicking water at him. "Maybe *you* should learn how to wash the floor."

She looked so absolutely, indignantly adorable that

he punched his hand into the bucket and splashed some water on her.

Her mouth rounded. "Just because your hand's bigger..." She took a good wave at the water and splashed enough on him to wet his shirt. Moments later they were both laughing as each got wetter. Eve's top clung to her breasts, and Hunter could see that she wasn't wearing a bra.

"I think you forgot to put something on this morning," he said, his heart pounding.

"I was hot," she responded breathlessly.

The two of them were on their knees facing each other. "As hot as you are now?" he asked.

"No. I'm much hotter right now."

The power of desire flashing through his veins was too overwhelming to deny. Reaching out, he traced her breasts with his fingers. Her eyes widened and her lips parted.

He did it again, slowly, with great deliberateness. Her tongue came out and licked her lips, and he wanted to taste them, too. Leaning toward her, he did, teasing her bottom lip with his tongue, then her upper lip, then lifting her shirt until his hands were covering both of her breasts. He heard the soft moan in her throat and played with her nipples until her tongue chased his and then she drew on him.

She was becoming bolder, and he liked it. Grasping handfuls of his shirt, she pulled it out of his shorts. They were unmindful of the mess they'd made with the water and the suds. Hunter didn't know anything except his need for Eve, the heat of their bodies, the pleasure he was ready to take.

When Eve hiked up his shirt, he tossed it over his

head. Then he drew hers up, off and tossed it aside, too. As her hand went to the button on his shorts, he was pulling hers down.

They disrobed in a matter of seconds and Hunter realized something. "We're going to slip and slide all over this damn floor."

When she laughed, her laughter soothed something in his soul.

Standing, he pulled her up and lifted her onto the island worktable in the center of the kitchen. Her gray eyes simmered with the desire he felt, and he said thickly, "Open your legs to me."

As she did, he gripped her buttocks, so firm yet so soft and feminine, and pulled her toward him. Then he entered her with a prolonged slowness, with a sensuality that took their breaths away.

"Oh, Hunter," Eve murmured.

"Tell me, Eve. Tell me how I make you feel."

"You make me feel..." She stopped.

He stroked in and out. "Tell me."

"You make me feel wanted and feminine and like everything in the universe is going to shatter around us."

When he thrust harder and deeper, she wrapped her legs around him. He kissed her, not interrupting their cadence, taking them both exactly where they wanted to go until the universe did burst and the earth moved and the bells rang....

Hunter shuddered into Eve and a minute later realized the bells weren't in his head, but in the foyer. It was the door chimes, and they were ringing again. He dropped his head to Eve's shoulder for a minute. "I don't know if the timing's good or bad."

Eve giggled. "If anyone ever knew what just happened in here—"

"Your disguise as a proper Southern lady would be right out the window." Hunter separated from her. "I'd better get it before whoever it is comes around back."

His feet sloshing into the puddles they'd made when they'd splashed each other, he reached for his shorts, pulled them on swiftly and zippered them. Still in his bare feet, trying to clear his head from the passion he'd just shared with his wife, he grabbed a towel from the refrigerator handle, wiped off his feet, then went to answer the door.

To his surprise, he found his father, who looked over the water-spotted shorts and his bare chest and feet.

"Is this a bad time?" John asked.

"Uh, no. We just had a mess in the kitchen and we're cleaning it up. What can I do for you?"

"If you're busy with something…"

"No. Come on in, I'll tell Eve you're here." That would send her scurrying to the laundry room for fresh clothes.

"I'd like to see Eve, too, of course, but…I came to talk to you."

The seriousness in his father's tone concerned Hunter, and he motioned him to the formal living room away from the family room and the kitchen. After Hunter had spoken to his dad about his health several weeks ago, he'd called Jolene to tell her nothing seemed to be wrong. But now…

John sat in the swan-armed upholstered rocker in front of the window.

Hunter settled in the blue-and-rose-velvet armchair and waited for the older man to say what he had come to say. But it wasn't anything Hunter expected when John began with, "I need your help on something."

Hunter waited.

"You know I'm grooming Larry to handle the company next year when I retire." He watched Hunter carefully.

"Yes, I know that."

"I've been trying to stand back and let him take over slowly, and he's doing a good job of it. But he wants to merge Morgan's Office Products with Otis Farley's chain of stores. Larry says mergers are the wave of the future, and it's the only way to grow our company dramatically."

Involved in mergers and acquisitions much of the time, Hunter knew that was partially true. "You don't think that's the way to go?"

"A merger is one thing. Otis Farley's company is another. I've heard rumors."

"What type of rumors?"

"Maybe *problems* is more the word I want. Distribution problems, sales force problems, maybe even financial problems. I'd like you to check them out."

Hunter knew Larry wouldn't want his interference. "Have you expressed your concerns to Larry?"

"I've expressed them, all right, but Larry just brushes them off. You know how headstrong he is, and he's forging ahead too fast. I don't want to see my life's work go up in smoke."

Hunter knew his father had worked hard to make his company successful. "What kind of information do you want?"

John Morgan shook his head, then shrugged. "I don't know exactly. Maybe I just want reassurance. I want to make sure Otis Farley's company is solid and we're not stepping into some kind of mud bog."

"This isn't exactly my field."

"I know, but you hear things and you have lots of contacts."

Yes, he did. "Is this the real reason you haven't been sleeping at night?"

John's face flushed. "Yes, and it's been causing me plenty of heartburn, too. I didn't want to involve you in this. I didn't want Larry to think I was looking over his shoulder."

"What if he finds out I'm doing this?"

"I'm sure he will eventually. We'll deal with it then. Your mom and I have worked hard to get to where we are now. When I retire, I'd like to take her on a trip or two. Maybe one of those cruises. I want to show her things she's never seen. When I asked her to marry me, I promised I'd provide for her and give her a good life."

"You've done that."

"Maybe so, but I want our last years together to be more comfortable than the rest...less work and more fun. That can't happen unless I'm sure Larry knows what he's doing."

"All right. I'll see what I can do. How soon do you need to know?"

"Larry's not planning to close the deal till fall, so we've got some time. Thank you, Hunter. This means a lot to me."

Eve appeared in the archway just then, and Hunter didn't have to respond.

She welcomed John with a wide smile. "Hi, there. Can you stay for lunch?"

John checked his watch. "I suppose I can. Martha went shopping with Jolene. When they go to a mall, I know they'll be gone all day."

"Good, then you can join us. I'm going to mix up a batch of lemonade, then we can eat out on the patio."

"No more iced tea left?" Hunter asked wickedly, noticing Eve had changed clothes. He guessed she was also now wearing a bra.

She wrinkled her nose at him. "The next time I make iced tea, I'll have to make a double batch."

He bit back a smile, thinking of what they'd shared in the kitchen, liking the idea of having intimate secrets with her. He felt almost happy. It was a new feeling and he didn't want to examine it too closely.

When Lauren MacMillan arrived on Monday afternoon, Eve was weeding the front flower bed bordering the house. She'd been so tired lately that she thought the fresh air and the sun might do her good. She certainly hadn't done anything strenuous at work this morning, mostly just taking inventory and helping a few customers.

Yesterday she'd asked Hunter to go along to church with her in the morning and he had. Afterward they'd packed up a picnic lunch and gone canoeing on a nearby lake. Hunter had done all the work. She'd gotten him to talk about some of the trips he'd taken and the sights he'd seen. He'd also told her all about Slade and Emily's ranch, the Double Blaze, in Montana. Last evening, they'd come home and made love for a good long time. That was when she felt the closest to Hunter.

Thinking about Saturday in their kitchen still made her smile.

Lauren pulled into the driveway and parked the white pickup truck with MacMillan's Garden Center painted in red on the door. After she climbed out, she saw Eve and waved. Then she crossed the yard with quick, long strides, a notebook in her hand.

"You're doing the hard part," Lauren said with a smile.

Eve laughed. "Hunter said a few tons of mulch will help with the weeds."

Appraising the grounds, Lauren asked, "Do you have any particular place you want me to start?"

"The front yard. Then we'll go around back and I'll show you the patio area and where I'd like to put the rock garden." The sun shone brightly as Eve shaded her eyes against it and looked up at Lauren.

"That sounds good," the landscape architect said, taking a few steps back to look more carefully at the front of the house. "I like the arborvitae that are already there. You can add one or two of the unusual sculptured evergreens, perhaps those geraniums you were looking at the other day interspersed with Shasta daisies."

Already Eve was visualizing the front yard. Color, contrast and freshness. Knowing exactly where she'd like to put the sculptured evergreens, she quickly scrambled to her feet. But she was overcome by a bout of dizziness that made her kneel back down again.

Lauren had glanced her way and now came rushing over. "Are you okay?"

Eve's head spun as it had on Saturday when she'd dropped the pitcher of iced tea. "I don't know what's wrong. This happened on Saturday, too. Maybe I have a touch of the flu."

Lauren crouched down beside her. "Or maybe too much sun. Have you been drinking enough?"

"I think so. Maybe I'm not eating enough. I haven't been very hungry."

Looking at her speculatively, Lauren gently took her arm. "Let's try this again. Slowly."

Eve took her time getting to her feet. The dizziness had faded as they'd talked and now she felt fine. "Maybe a glass of water would be a good idea. Do you have time to sit for a few minutes?"

"Sure. I've been on the run since six o'clock this morning."

Eve left her gardening gloves and tools, and they went in the front door. After she'd gotten herself a glass of water and poured Lauren a tumbler of iced tea, they took their drinks out back and sat on the patio.

"How are you feeling?" Lauren asked.

"Fine, now."

"I know it's none of my business, but could you be pregnant?"

Eve felt thunderstruck as she thought about the past two weeks. The lack of appetite usually began with mild nausea in the morning. She hadn't thought much about it, since so much had changed about her life recently. She'd thought she was just having trouble keeping up. But now that Lauren had suggested it...

She broke into a smile. "It's possible, though I hadn't expected it to happen so fast."

"From what I understand, it only takes once," Lauren remarked casually.

Something in Lauren's voice made Eve look at her closely.

Lauren was flushed, and it had nothing to do with the weather. "I shouldn't have said anything," she mumbled. "I wouldn't know anything about it."

Always taught to tread delicately, Eve asked, "You're not dating someone?"

Lauren gave a vigorous shake of her head. "Too busy for that."

Eve suspected there were reasons other than just busyness. "Too busy...or waiting for the right man."

"I'm not so sure I'd know the right man if he came along. There was someone once—" She stopped abruptly.

Eve said with a kind smile, "A woman as attractive as you could be dating anybody."

Lauren leaned back in her chair. "I like you."

"I like you, too," Eve said, meaning it. "Maybe we could have lunch together sometime...or dinner. Hunter often works late."

"Sure. That would be nice." She picked up her notebook. "Why don't you stay here and rest, and I'll make some diagrams of the front yard and come back here. Then we'll talk."

Eve nodded.

As Lauren rounded the corner of the yard, Eve sank back into the pillows on the lawn chair and said a prayer of gratitude toward heaven. Not only might she be pregnant, but she'd made her first new friend, too.

And she couldn't wait to see Hunter to tell him about both.

* * *

But Eve didn't see Hunter that evening. He called to tell her he had a meeting and would be late getting home. She tried to wait up for him, but fell asleep with her book on her lap. In the morning he was up early and had left before she awakened. So she decided to buy a home pregnancy test to make sure they were going to have a baby before she said anything about it.

On her way home from the gallery, Eve stopped at a drugstore and bought the test. When she used it, she found she was indeed pregnant. Going downstairs, she set the dining-room table for two with her mother's china. After she put tapers in the sterling silver candleholders that had been a wedding present, she went to the kitchen and took out her favorite cookbook. She wanted to make something really special.

Deciding on a London broil with onion sauce, she set about making dessert first. She had plenty of lemons, and a lemon meringue pie would be a perfect dessert. After Hunter enjoyed that, she'd tell him her news.

The lemon pie was cooling on a rack on the counter and she was about ready to pound the meat when Hunter phoned. "I have a favor to ask," he said.

"What?"

"There's a cocktail party tonight, and I can't miss it. A few of my clients and their wives will be there. I'd like you to come with me."

She looked at the pie and the meat. "This is important?"

"I think so. The problem is, I won't be able to get

home before the party. Can you meet me there? I'll send a car for you.''

"You don't have to do that. I can drive in.''

"That's not a good idea. You'd have to drive through a bad part of town. I'll send the car about seven.''

"I'll be ready.''

"Thanks, Eve.''

He sounded as if she was doing him a favor. Couldn't he tell yet that she loved being with him? That she'd do anything for him?

Two hours later, Eve walked into the reception area of a lavish suite of offices in a downtown Denver office building. The driver of the car had escorted her up the elevator to the eighth floor and shown her where to go. As she threaded through the crowd of people, looking for Hunter, she saw everything from sequins to short black knit dresses on the women, but mostly tailor-made suits on the men. She guessed this was an elite crowd, and she hoped she looked as if she fit in. She'd worn a black-and-white sheath with a three-tiered flounce at the hem of the skirt. The bands of white against black were striking. She hadn't worn this dress in a long time. For an evening look, she'd piled her hair high on top of her head in a loose bed of curls, hoping they'd stay put for the evening. Hunter had once told her he liked it that way.

Finally she spotted Hunter speaking with a group of men in one corner. She didn't want to intrude, but she did want to let him know that she was there. She couldn't wait to tell him her news.

A waiter stepped in her path and offered her a glass of wine, but she declined. As she looked again to the corner of the room, she saw a woman in a beaded, champagne-colored dress that didn't cover much of anything sidle up to Hunter. It was the woman in the newspaper photograph. He bent toward her to listen, and his ear was much too close to her mouth. There wasn't *that* much noise in the room, Eve thought.

She stood watching for a few moments, saw Hunter nod, then give the woman a smile. The blonde was fluttering her lashes at him, doing that thing women do with their eyes when they're flirting...and this lady was flirting big-time. Hunter's shoulder was brushing the blonde's bare one, and Eve didn't like the familiarity she sensed between them.

Did Hunter intend to be faithful to his wedding vows? Or would he tire of being a one-woman man? What would happen as her pregnancy progressed? What would happen when she got fat? Would he look in other directions for the kind of sex they'd had in the kitchen on Saturday?

Suddenly too many doubts to count plagued her and she knew why. He never shared his feelings with her. He never told her he was happy or sad or worried. He never told her how much he cared.

Her conscience whispered, *Have you told him?*

No, she hadn't. But she did try to share everything about her day, her pleasure in making a home for them, the fun of creating gardens, her excitement and contentment at how he made her feel when they went to bed. She hadn't told him she loved him because she didn't think he could accept that yet, and she didn't want him brushing it off as something she didn't mean or something she said because she should.

Still, she wasn't going to stand here and watch that blonde pretend that she belonged with Hunter.

Taking a deep breath, Eve walked forward, putting what she hoped was a serene smile on her face. She didn't sidle up to Hunter as the blonde had done. Rather, she waved at him as she approached, and then stood across from him in the midst of the men.

"I found you," she said, happiness evident in her voice that she had. "Thank you for sending the car for me. That way we can drive home together."

The three men and the blonde standing there looked at Eve speculatively, and then stared at Hunter.

His expression unreadable, Hunter said easily, "David, Adam, Charles and Barbara, this is my wife, Eve."

"What?"

Eve ignored the exclamation from Barbara and extended a hand to each of the men and then to her, too. Barbara looked at it as if she didn't know what to do with it but finally gave it a quick shake.

"It's so good to meet all of you," Eve commented.

The man Eve remembered as Charles spoke up first. "I saw that ring on Hunter's hand, but he didn't mention a wife. How long have you two been married?"

When Eve didn't respond right away, Hunter did. "About six weeks."

Barbara's eyes narrowed and Eve could feel the daggers, though the men were smiling pleasantly at her, almost appreciatively.

Adam said, "I'll go find Marge, and you can introduce Eve to her. I bet she'd love to have you two over for dinner." He stepped away to find his wife.

"You'll have to join us on the boat some weekend," Charles added. "I'm sure Claudia would like to get to know Eve as well. She's not here tonight, unfortunately. She had one of those organizational meetings at one of the charities she sponsors."

"You have a boat?" Eve asked.

Charles launched into an explanation of not only the type of boat, but its appointments as well. As Eve kept asking questions, Charles kept elucidating.

Barbara started to look bored. Hooking her arm through Hunter's, she asked, "Why don't we go have another glass of wine?"

But Eve took that opportunity to say to Charles, "I hope my husband has the time tonight to introduce me to more of his colleagues." Out of the corner of her eye, she saw Hunter disengage his arm from Barbara's.

"Charles, Barbara, David, it was good talking to you, but I see Adam waving to us and I'd like to introduce Eve around." With that, Hunter moved toward her, laid a hand protectively at the small of her back and guided her to another part of the room.

As they walked, he murmured, "You're smooth."

"I beg your pardon?"

"You're good, Eve. Charles loves talking about that boat, and you picked up on that right away."

Yes, she had. And she'd sensed something else, too. "Have you ever been on his boat?"

Hunter frowned. "No."

"But now that you're married, he's going to invite you?"

"It sure sounds like it, doesn't it? I've never been invited to Adam and Marge's for dinner before, either."

Eve stopped walking. "It looks as if marriage has given you access to situations and people you wouldn't otherwise have."

Hunter looked uncomfortable. "It's a nice by-product of being married. You're a charming woman, Eve, and I knew you'd be an asset."

An asset.

Unreasonable anger surfaced, and she knew it had something to do with the jealousy she'd felt at seeing Barbara's interaction with her husband. "I'm glad you find me valuable in this capacity," she said coolly.

"Eve..." Hunter began impatiently.

She started walking away from him, but he clasped her elbow. "I don't know why you're miffed. *You* married *me* to get your inheritance."

Chapter Seven

The look in Eve's eyes told Hunter that was the wrong thing to say right here, right now, even though it had been the truth. He was sure of it when she pulled out of his grasp and headed for the door.

But on her way there, Adam intercepted her, introducing her to his wife. A few moments later Hunter joined them, perturbed with Eve because she unsettled him so…because her beauty aroused him. Watching her, he was taken again by her charm and her way with people. Her reentrance into his life had disturbed him, until things that used to make sense didn't make sense anymore.

They got caught up in one conversation after another and the direction of the evening marched right out of Hunter's hands. Instead of enriching his already elite client base, he found himself simply enjoying watching Eve interact. She was striking in that dress and so gracious to everyone with whom she came into contact that they wanted to monopolize her for the evening. Nodding acquaintances of Hunter's asked for introductions, looking disappointed when they discovered Hunter and Eve were married.

Finally guests began dispersing, and Hunter found Charles to thank him for the invitation to the party. Afterward, he found Eve involved in a conversation with a group of women.

As he approached them, he heard one of them say to her, "You must join our garden club."

His hand resting possessively on her waist, Hunter stood close to her. "If you ladies don't mind, I'm going to spirit my wife away."

Adam's wife said with a sly smile, "We understand completely. It was so good to meet you, Eve. I'll give you a call about the garden club luncheon."

Eve looked up at him and smiled, but he could tell it was forced.

After they said their goodbyes, they took the elevator to the parking garage. Hunter drove out of the garage into the main flow of traffic. When they stopped at a red light, he asked Eve, "Did you enjoy yourself?"

"Most of the time I did. I recognized a few of the people there from our wedding."

He wished she didn't sound so...so...

He wasn't sure what it was, but he suspected something was on her mind. A moment later he found out what.

"Was that Barbara's nightgown I found in the guest room drawer?"

How did women *know* these things? "Does it matter?"

"That depends. You said you weren't involved with anyone before we got married."

"I wasn't. Barbara and I dated a few times, that's all."

"Dated?" Eve asked, giving him a skeptical look.

"I'm not sure what you're getting at, Eve, but if you're worried about my past partners, I've always been exceptionally careful, except for that one time in Savannah with you."

The light turned green, and he stepped on the accelerator.

After a stretch of uncomfortable quiet, Eve fiddled with her seat belt. "Did Barbara know you weren't 'involved' with her?"

"I don't even know why we're having this conversation," he grumbled. He and Barbara had been two consenting adults who'd taken pleasure with each other twice. That was it. He'd known it, and Barbara had known it. She was a no-strings, just-have-fun type of woman.

"We're having this conversation," Eve said evenly, "because I'd like to know if whatever was between the two of you is finished."

"I married *you*. It's finished. It was finished before you arrived in Denver."

"Is she still your client?"

"Yes. We're adults, Eve. I handle negotiations for her company. That's all."

Silence lay heavy between them as he drove the rest of the way home, pushed the button on the garage door opener and headed inside. Eve preceded Hunter through the mudroom and down the hall into the kitchen.

When he saw the pie sitting on the counter, he stopped. "What's that?"

"Lemon meringue pie."

He could see into the dining room, where he glimpsed the place settings for two, as well as the tapers in the candleholders. "What *is* all this? Candles, dessert...?"

"I had planned a special dinner."

There was a slight quiver in her voice and her eyes were shiny. "I had some news to tell you and I wanted everything to be...well...perfect."

He felt his breath lodge in his chest as he took a few steps closer to her. "What news?"

"I'm pregnant, Hunter."

It took a moment for her words to register. When they did, he felt such a rush of joy, he asked eagerly, "Really? Your doctor said there wouldn't be a problem, but I—"

"My doctor? When did you talk to my doctor?"

"Before we left Savannah. You told me that I could call him to confirm that you could get pregnant again."

"You didn't trust me," she said, her voice trembling.

"I needed to make sure. You hadn't told me about the pregnancy, the miscarriage—"

Eve walked away from him toward the stairs.

Catching up to her, he clasped her shoulder. "Eve."

There were tears in her eyes when she turned toward him. "I wish you could trust me."

Would he ever be able to trust her? Once he had trusted her with everything he was, and she'd handed it back to him. But now she was going to have his baby. "Eve, we're pregnant. That's all that matters."

She looked deep into his eyes. "This baby is very important to you, isn't it?"

"Yes. We'll have a family, Eve. We'll *be* a family."

"And to you that means everything," she murmured.

"Not everything," he responded, a combination of joy and desire making his voice husky.

When he lifted her chin, she gazed up at him with a longing he couldn't understand. He wanted her and she wanted him. And together they had created a new life.

He drew her close to him and kissed her with all the gratitude he felt, with all the promise a child could bring. Eve responded with fervent passion. He swung her into his arms, then carried her up the stairs.

A long while later, Eve awakened. Hunter's arm was around her and she lay curled against his shoulder. He'd made sweet, tender love to her.

It had been such a mixed-up evening—happiness and jealousy, disappointment and passion. Hunter was so thrilled with the idea of being a father. Yet he didn't trust her. He didn't realize she'd married him for a much more important reason than her inheritance. She loved him, but if he didn't trust her, he'd never trust her words. Somehow she had to prove to him that he was the most important person in her life...that he *was* her life.

Suddenly, his voice deep and husky, Hunter asked, "Are you awake?"

"I'm awake."

"I've been thinking about all the ways we have to get ready. Do you want to redo one of the guest bedrooms?"

"That would be nice. I've noticed lots of adorable children's wallpapers."

Stroking her hair, he asked, "How much notice will you give the gallery that you're leaving?"

She tilted her head back. "The baby isn't due for almost eight months. It's a little early to think about that."

"You're going to keep working?"

"Sure. Why shouldn't I?"

"You need to take care of yourself, Eve."

She knew he was thinking about her miscarriage, and she was, too. A stark fear shot through her. What if she miscarried again? What would happen to their marriage then? But she had to think positively. She had to hope for the best.

"I like working at the gallery, Hunter. With you gone for such long hours, it gives me something to do. I need to feel productive, just as you do."

"Promise me if it gets to be too taxing, you'll quit."

"I promise."

"Once the baby's born, I'll cut back on my hours. I want to be a 'real' father."

She wished he was around more now. When he wasn't, she had doubts he'd ever let her get close. She often went into the room with her father's paintings, asked him if she'd done the right thing by marrying Hunter, and let grief-filled tears fall. Sometimes she thought she heard her father's voice telling her to give Hunter time.

Time.

She wished she and Hunter could spend more of it together. But the purpose of this marriage, as Hunter saw it, was to have children and give them a good life. What he didn't realize was that, to make the rest of their world secure, children needed two parents who loved each other.

The headquarters for Morgan's Office Products was located in Aurora, a suburb of Denver. Hunter had telephoned John Morgan this morning to tell him what he'd discovered about Otis Farley and his company, and John had asked him to speak to Larry personally. It wasn't something Hunter relished doing, but his father never asked him for favors and this seemed like a small one. Now Hunter hoped to catch Larry off guard so he'd listen to what he had to say.

The Morgan's Office Products complex was situated on a small parcel of land in an unobtrusive building covered with brown siding. Hunter smiled at the receptionist, who knew him, and told her he was there to see his brother and he'd go on back. She nodded agreeably. Hunter passed the suites of the account managers and the sales force. Knowing his father was meeting an old friend for lunch today, Hunter passed his office and stopped before Larry's.

He rapped, and his brother called, "Come in."

Larry's desk was cluttered with papers, and so was every other available surface in his office. The computer was on and he was making notes on a legal pad. When he looked up and saw Hunter, he frowned.

"Are you here to see Dad?" Larry asked. "He's off for the afternoon."

"Actually I came to see you." Hunter stepped into the office and closed the door.

Larry noted it and his eyes narrowed. "Is this business or personal?"

"Does it matter?" Hunter asked lightly, trying to keep the usual tension from cropping up between them, trying to keep peace.

"I'm busy," Larry snapped.

Hunter nodded. "I can see that."

"Don't look down your nose at me, Hunter. Just because my office isn't as plush as yours doesn't mean I don't get my share of work done. In fact, I probably do more."

The hostility in Larry's voice always surprised Hunter. He constantly hoped it wouldn't be there. He constantly hoped something would change between them. But that hope had died over the years and now he just tried to be civil.

"I didn't come here to compare our workloads. I wanted to discuss the merger you're planning."

Defensive before, now Larry straightened his shoulders, and his mouth became a tight, firm line. Finally he asked, "Did Dad ask you to talk to me?"

"He asked me to look into Otis Farley and his company."

Larry stood. "I don't appreciate either one of you trying to second-guess me."

Hunter stayed seated and stayed calm. "Dad's concerned, that's all."

"Concerned? I don't think so. He knows I'm capable of handling his business. I've been practically doing it all for the past five years. Now suddenly I want to turn it into something bigger and better, and he runs to you."

"I didn't come here to argue with you, Larry. Dad asked me to look into Otis Farley's background, so that's what I did. Farley attempted to merge with companies twice last year, and both times the deals fell through."

"That happens," Larry said, as if it were elementary.

"Yes, it does. But the year before that, the stock buyback plan he initiated also fell through and several members of his board resigned. I don't think you're dealing with a stable organization."

"I don't give a fig in hell what you think. This deal has nothing to do with you. It's *my* future and *my* success that's involved, and I want you to keep *your* nose out of it. Did you tell all this crap to Dad?"

"He asked me what I found out."

"And you couldn't wait to give him tidbits that mean absolutely nothing. Listen, Hunter, I'm not going to let you make me look bad. I'm not going to let you ruin a deal that could set me and my family up for life. If you want to play private investigator, fine. Do it on your time and with your clients. Just stay clear of what I'm trying to accomplish here."

The things Hunter had discovered about Otis Farley had sent up red flags. He didn't have anything concrete, just rumors, situations that by themselves meant nothing. But intuition had told him he smelled a rat. Yet if Larry wouldn't listen to him, there wasn't anything more he could do.

Standing, he buttoned his suit coat and went to the door. "Dad asked me to tell you what I'd learned. I have. If you want to ignore the warning signs, there's nothing I can do about that.'' Then he opened the door and left his brother's office.

Hunter hurried down the hall eager to leave the building that for years had reminded him that his father had chosen Larry to be the Morgans' banner carrier. John Morgan had never discussed or asked Hunter if he wanted to be part of the family business. Maybe it was Hunter's own fault for staying secluded when he was a teenager, concentrating on sports and studies, telling himself he didn't care if he didn't fit in anywhere. He'd written for college catalogs on his own, and one day had shown them to his parents, telling them he intended to be a lawyer. What if, instead, he had told John Morgan he wanted to work beside him in the family business?

Then there would have been even more tension with Larry, which would have raised the rivalry between them to unbelievable levels. Hunter hadn't thought *that* would be good for anyone.

Now as he left the building, the worry in his father's voice as he'd talked about his life's work disturbed Hunter. Even though he knew he should, he couldn't let this go. Rumors and failed deals weren't enough to make Larry listen. But what if Hunter got some kind of concrete proof? What if Otis Farley's books didn't match his financial reports? What if he engaged in business practices that undercut the company's reliability?

Hunter thought about a friend of his, Simon Albright, who did consulting work to businesses for security reasons. Maybe Simon could get Hunter something on paper, something that Larry couldn't dispute, something that undeniably showed him this merger was bad for Morgan's Office Products.

With new resolve, Hunter strode across the parking lot to his car. He had to do everything he could to save his father's company for him because maybe if he did...

He'd feel like a "real" son.

On his way back to his office, Hunter thought about the child Eve was carrying and a broad smile turned up his lips. At the same time, he was passing a shopping center and saw the toy store. Impulsively, he turned on his signal and decided to go in.

An hour later, he carried two large bags into his new home and called, "Eve?"

Coming out of the kitchen, she stopped when she saw him. "I just tried to call you at your office. Slade, Emily, Mark and Amanda are coming for a visit next week."

"That's great. I can't wait for you to meet them. I know you'll like them."

"I hope I can get everything ready in time."

"What's to get ready?"

"Hunter! We're having guests. I have to make sure we have enough guest towels, that the rooms are clean, plan our meals..."

"Whoa," he said, putting one bag on the low coffee table in the family room. "Slade and Emily won't expect you to go to a lot of trouble, and they won't sit back and let you do everything. And as far as meals go, we can always eat out."

"You've told me that Emily's quite a homemaker. I want to make sure everything's just right."

Hunter tipped Eve's chin up and kissed her. "It will

be," he murmured. Maybe coming home in the middle of the afternoon wasn't such a bad idea. "We could go upstairs and look at what I bought," he said in a low voice.

"We could," she drawled. "But if we do, the cake I have in the oven will probably burn." She peeked into the bag still in his arm, but when she lifted out a fluffy white teddy bear, she wasn't smiling.

"It looks as if you've been shopping."

"The store called out to me on the way home." As he emptied the rest of the bag onto the table, rattles, a ball and a stuffed green dinosaur spilled out. "I couldn't resist. And you know what? I think we ought to go shopping for baby furniture tonight."

"I work tonight," she said quietly. "I was making a cake so we could have it with strawberries and whipped cream when I get home."

"You could call in sick," he suggested, half seriously, half not.

"No, I can't, Hunter. There's no one to cover for me."

"Then why don't we go shopping for furniture now?"

"After the cake comes out, I have to take a shower and get dressed. Besides, we shouldn't shop for furniture until after we redo the room."

Was she stalling him for some reason? "What's the matter, Eve?"

"Nothing's the matter."

"Don't lie to me."

Her face paled. "I'm not lying, Hunter. I just..." She waved her hand over the coffee table and the toys there.

"I just don't know if this is a good idea. I don't know if shopping for anything right now is a good idea."

"Why not?"

"What if…" She hesitated a moment. "What if I have another miscarriage?"

Ever since she'd told him she was pregnant, he'd felt ten feet tall. He'd felt as if his life was coming together. "You won't."

"Hunter…"

"Is there something you're not telling me?"

"No!"

"Did you make an appointment with a doctor?"

"Yes. I called someone your mother recommended, and I'm going in next week."

"Then why are you worried?"

"Because if it happened once, it can happen again."

"It won't happen again. It might not have happened the first time if you'd contacted me, if you'd taken care of yourself."

"Hunter!"

There was a hurt look in her eyes, but he couldn't deny the way he felt. He couldn't deny the fact that he blamed her for the miscarriage.

"The doctor told me that the miscarriage happened because it wasn't meant to be," she said defensively.

"That was a platitude," he fired back, finally letting the bitterness out.

She took a step back away from him. "You know better than a doctor?"

"I know that he was trying to make you feel better. You'd rather believe it was fate than something you did." He couldn't keep the resentment from his voice.

"This time I want you to take care of yourself. I want you to eat right, get plenty of rest, and if your job interferes with your health, I think you should quit."

She shook her head and insisted, "My job isn't interfering with my health. It's giving me something worthwhile to do. You know how I love art. You know how I love working with paintings and sculptures."

He remembered the other evening when he'd found her standing in the room surrounded by her father's art collection. She'd been crying, and he'd supposed it was because she missed her dad. He'd walked away without letting her know he was there.

"You can appreciate art from here. I don't like your driving home alone at night."

As the buzzer sounded on the stove, Eve looked over her shoulder. "I have to take the cake out."

She still looked hurt, and he didn't know what to do with the anger that he felt about her losing their baby. He still didn't believe she'd tried to contact him. He didn't believe she'd wanted that baby half as much as he had.

Gathering up the toys, he pushed them back into the bag. "I'll put these upstairs in one of the guest rooms until you're ready to shop for furniture. How long do we have to wait, Eve? Three months? Five months? Seven months? What's the magic number?"

The timer kept up its insistent buzzing.

"Let's at least give it a few months. The first trimester."

Avoiding looking at her, he said, "Fine. The first trimester it is. Maybe I should go along with you to the doctor's next week. Then we can both have all our questions answered."

He didn't wait for her to agree or to protest. He was going to make damn sure she took care of herself, that they did everything necessary to ensure this pregnancy would be a healthy one.

Lifting the bags, he headed for the stairs.

On Saturday afternoon the baseball glanced off Mark's bat, skidded by Slade, who was pitching to his son, and came toward Hunter. Hunter scooped it up with his glove and called, "Great hit, Mark."

The eight-year-old ran over to Hunter. "Is it okay if I go in for a drink, Uncle Hunter? I'm awfully thirsty."

It was a hot day and the three of them had been playing ball for the past half hour. "Sure, go ahead. If you want a snack, I'm sure Eve can find a chocolate chip cookie or two."

Slade told Mark, "Just remember to say *please* and *thank-you.*"

Mark nodded and ran into the house.

Hunter studied his twin. He and Slade were fraternal twins, but they looked alike except for their hair color. Slade's was brown. "He's a great kid," Hunter said, as they walked toward the patio.

"He sure is. He teaches me something new every day, and now you have that to look forward to."

The thrill of becoming a father practically over-whelmed Hunter, and he'd told Slade and Emily about it soon after they'd arrived. But the thrill was tempered by a tinge of fear that everything would not go well in Eve's pregnancy. "I can't wait."

Slade took the baseball from Hunter's hand and tossed it lightly up into the air. Then he took a long look at his brother. "Are you going to tell me what's going on between you and Eve?"

He wasn't sure himself what was going on. Things had been tense for the past week, ever since the afternoon he'd come home with the toys. That night they'd realized seven-month-old Amanda would need a place to sleep, and Hunter had bought a portable crib that he had told Eve they could use downstairs after their baby was born. She hadn't objected.

"We didn't marry for the usual reasons," he admitted.

Slade waited for him to explain.

"Eve and I knew each other five years ago. I asked her to marry me and she said no. But after her father died a few months ago, she discovered his will had an unusual provision. She wouldn't inherit his estate unless she married within a year. She came to me and asked me if I'd marry her. I decided we could both get something we wanted. She'd get her inheritance, and I'd get a family."

After turning the baseball around in his hand, Slade walked to the edge of the flagstones, stepping into the shade of the latticework there. "So you two have a history."

"Yes." Then Hunter told Slade that Eve had gotten pregnant five years ago and miscarried.

"You don't seem as happy as a new bridegroom should be. Now I can see why."

"I thought this would be easier," Hunter confessed. "I thought looking forward and not back could get us both what we wanted."

"Maybe you have to forgive what's back there before you can move forward."

Hunter didn't have time to think about Slade's advice, let alone respond, because the back door opened. Eve came out with a tray holding two glasses of lemonade and a dish of chocolate chip cookies.

"Can you use something to drink?"

Smiling at her, Slade answered, "Sure can. You're taking good care of us."

Emily and Slade had arrived three days ago and Eve had insisted on cooking for them every night. She'd also planned a party for tomorrow and invited the Morgan clan. Setting the tray on the glass patio table, Eve told Slade, "I'm enjoying it."

Slade glanced down at the dish of cookies. "I'm going in to wash up before I dig in to them. Be right back."

Breaking the silence that had settled between the two of them more often than not lately, she said, "You're good with Mark."

"He's a terrific kid."

"Emily told me he started calling Slade *Dad* right after their wedding."

"The two of you seem to be hitting it off," Hunter remarked.

"I like Emily a lot, and I admire her. She ran that ranch by herself before Slade came along. She told me how Slade helped deliver Amanda."

Hunter had been watching Eve with the seven-month-old baby and she seemed to be enjoying taking care of Amanda to give Emily a break. This morning he'd found Eve rocking her while Emily was taking a shower. The vision of Eve and the baby had caused his chest to tighten, and he'd imagined her holding their child.

"Are you hoping for a boy or girl?" Eve asked softly.

When he looked down at her, he realized he needed something he couldn't quite name, and he decided it was the birth of their child. "I'd like a boy to carry on the Coleburn name, but...I think about having a little girl, too. So I guess it really doesn't matter. What about you?"

Eve laid her hand protectively over her stomach. "It doesn't matter. I'm looking forward to either, to everything about having a child."

Eve's eyes were bright with hope, and Hunter stepped closer to her. "Did you take your vitamins today?" He'd driven her to her first doctor's appointment yesterday.

"I'm taking care of myself, Hunter. This baby means as much to me as it does to you."

He wondered if that was possible. He wondered if raising a child together was the glue their marriage needed. He hoped and prayed that it was.

Chapter Eight

The party was a success, Eve thought, as she went into the kitchen to fill the warming tray with more hot hors d'oeuvres. Everyone was mingling and talking, and the food was disappearing fast. Larry's two children and Mark were playing a game in the family room while Amanda napped upstairs. As Eve took the tray of mini-quiches from the oven, she felt suddenly very weary. Since she'd become pregnant, that usually happened this time of day, and this week she hadn't had much time to rest.

Emily came into the kitchen carrying an empty platter. "I need more sandwich rolls. Do we have some?"

Emily Lawrence Coleburn was a dynamo, and even though she looked soft-spoken and delicate, she was as hardy as a pioneer woman. Still, she was Eve's guest. "You don't need to help. Just go enjoy yourself."

As Emily put more rolls on the platter, she glanced

at Eve. "You've been cooking for all of us since we arrived. I think you should let us all pitch in. I remember what it's like being pregnant and having household chores."

Eve had this idea that she could show Hunter that she loved him through everything she did. Welcoming his family into their house had become a mission for her. "I'm going to miss you when you leave on Tuesday. It's been nice having you here."

"You know, I was a little worried when Slade said we were going to stay with you, us being strangers and all. But you never seemed like a stranger."

Just then, Hunter walked in.

After she picked up the tray of rolls, Emily winked at Eve, and returned to the dining room.

"What are you and Emily cooking up?" he asked with a smile, looking more relaxed than Eve had seen him since she'd come to Denver. Slade seemed to have that effect on him.

"Not a thing. We're just busy feeding a hungry crowd."

As she transferred quiches onto the warming tray, he came to stand by her side. "Do you mind if I make an announcement about your pregnancy?"

She looked up at him and could see it was important to him. "No, I don't mind. I guess Slade and Emily have been keeping it quiet."

"I asked them to. I didn't know if you were ready to tell anyone else." She remembered the conversation about her fears, and the tension that had put between them. It had lessened since Slade and his family had been here. She still had fears, but she had a lot more hope.

"Would you like to do it now?"

Hunter's smile told her he would.

A short time later, he asked for everyone's attention as he and Eve stood together in front of the fireplace. "Eve and I have an announcement to make," he said proudly.

Martha's eyes grew big and John's expression looked expectant. Larry looked disinterested, but Jolene was smiling as if she'd guessed what it was.

"Eve and I are going to have a baby."

After Midge and Jolene congratulated them, Martha and John hugged them, murmuring how happy they were for them. Slade gave Hunter a thumbs-up sign and the two men exchanged a look only twins could share.

"Now the fun really starts," Larry said cynically. "I don't quite see Hunter as the changing-diapers kind of guy. Are you going to get a nanny?"

"There won't be any need for a nanny," Eve replied.

Slade strode over to stand beside his twin. "Hunter's been great with Mark and Amanda this week. I imagine he'll be even better with his own."

"Eve and I will probably attend childbirth and parenting courses. We'll be prepared," Hunter said.

Surprised, Eve looked up at him. "You mean that?"

"Sure. I'm going to give our child all the time he or she needs before, during and after birth."

Without thinking twice, Eve stood on tiptoe and kissed Hunter's cheek. He looked startled, then his arm went around her, and he kissed her full on the lips. She blushed until Martha asked, "Have you thought about names?"

"Not yet, but soon," Hunter said. He kept his arm around her, and Eve wished she could always feel the sense of belonging she felt at this moment.

As the evening wore on, Eve made another pot of coffee and cut the chocolate cake she'd made. She sat on the sofa beside Hunter, and her arm companionably brushed his every now and then. Their gazes caught and met often, and she wondered if he was getting past blaming her for her miscarriage. Neither of them had brought it up again.

Sitting in the rocker by the living-room window, Emily repositioned seven-month-old Amanda when she yawned. "I think this one's getting sleepy. I'm going to take her upstairs and get her ready for bed."

Eve asked, "Can I do it?" She'd helped Emily the past couple of nights and loved taking care of the little girl.

"Sure," Emily answered.

Standing, Eve crossed to the rocker and held her arms out to Amanda. Giving her a sleepy smile, the little girl leaned toward her and Eve gathered her up.

Eve had washed Amanda's face and hands and dressed her in her pj's by the time Emily came in and murmured, "I can take over now." Emily's eyes softened as she picked up her daughter, and Eve realized that though they'd been separated for only a short while, Emily had missed the baby.

When Eve returned downstairs, she went into the dining room to see if they needed more ice or refreshments. After she refilled the ice bucket, she poured herself a glass of lemonade.

Larry came in. "Nice party," he said with a wave at everything.

"Thank you."

"It looks as if you and Hunter have everything you could want."

She could hear a hint of jealousy in Larry's voice, and she said cautiously, "We're looking forward to raising a family."

"Yeah, well, maybe that will keep Hunter busier so he stays out of my affairs."

"I'm not sure I know what you mean."

"So you don't know he's trying to mess up my deal of a lifetime?"

Hunter hadn't said anything on the subject of Larry or his parents. But she knew one thing for certain. "I'm sure Hunter would never do anything intentionally to hurt you."

With a shake of his head, Larry grimaced. "Maybe you don't know your husband as well as you think. If you have any influence over him, tell him to stick to law and leave the family business to me."

Before she could question Larry further, he said, "I'm going to round up my wife and kids. I have a full day tomorrow."

Larry Morgan puzzled Eve. He was so different from both Hunter and Jolene. She suspected a deep insecurity made him obnoxious at times. No wonder Hunter kept his distance.

After everyone left, Eve loaded the dishwasher, feeling so tired she was almost nauseous. But she still had debris to gather up in the living room and family room.

Hunter came into the kitchen with the ice bucket and dumped the melting ice into the sink. "Slade and

Emily have taken Mark upstairs. I think everyone enjoyed themselves.''

"I think they did, too," Eve agreed absently, running her hand across her brow.

Hunter came over to her and tipped up her chin. "You look beat."

"I am. I guess parties can be more tiring than I thought."

"Why don't you go on up? I'll take care of the rest of this."

When she hesitated, he cupped her chin in his palm. "Go on. I'll be up shortly."

Too tired now to argue with him, she nodded. "I think I'll get a bath first, though. Thanks for finishing up for me."

"We're in this together, Eve."

She gazed into his eyes, wondering exactly what that meant to him—commitment, fidelity, loyalty...love?

Upstairs, she filled the sunken tub, adding bath crystals, a wonderful gardenia scent she always used. After the tub was full, she pinned up her hair and lowered herself into it, laying her head back against the edge and closing her eyes, thinking about Hunter and the baby inside her.

Someone was calling her name from a great distance. It sounded like Hunter's voice.

"Eve?"

Opening her eyes, she could see him crouched beside the tub, his hand in the water. "This is getting cold. I think you fell asleep in here."

"Mmm, could be," she murmured, trying to get

awake. But then she realized her husband wasn't wearing his sleeping shorts, and he was looking down at her breasts just under the surface of the water. All of the bubbles had disappeared. Although the water was tepid, it seemed warmer suddenly, and she brought herself to a sitting position, totally aware of Hunter's naked body as he looked down at her.

He took the fluffy, rose towel from where Eve had laid it on the white-and-gold bench and said, "Come on. Let's get you to bed."

She and Hunter had explored each other's bodies many times, but she still felt a little shy with him. Rising, she stepped out of the tub.

He hesitated only a moment before he wrapped the large towel around her and tucked it in at her breasts. Before she realized what he intended, he'd scooped her up into his arms and was carrying her into the bedroom.

"What are you doing?"

"I didn't want you to slip on the wet tile. You're not altogether awake."

She was fast becoming completely awake with her arms around his neck, her breast pressed against his bare chest.

When he laid her down on the bed, he asked, "Is there anything you need before I turn off the lights?"

Yes, she thought to herself. *You.* But she didn't say it, she just shook her head.

A few moments later he was in bed beside her. "Aren't you going to take the towel off?" he teased.

"I thought you might like to do that," she responded softly.

There was a moment of silence, and she wondered how she dared to be so brazen. It served her right if...

"I thought you were tired."

"I had a nap in the tub, remember?"

"I remember," he replied, his voice husky. Rolling to his side, he propped himself on an elbow, then trailed his finger along the edge of the towel. "I want to thank you," he said.

"For what?"

His finger teasing the edge of the towel distracted her. "For welcoming Slade and Emily into our home, for making their stay enjoyable. It's a real treat for Emily not to have to cook, or for her and Slade to get breaks from caring for the kids. She said she feels as if she's on vacation."

"She is. And she and Slade...they feel like family. Do you know what I mean?"

"Oh, yeah." He loosened the tuck of the towel. "You did a great job with the party, too."

"I enjoyed it." Her breath caught when he flipped the towel back and stared down at her.

"I think your breasts are fuller already." He bent and brushed a light kiss on one.

He was right. They were. And soon her waistline would change, too. In bed was the one place she and Hunter really connected. What would happen when her body was different? Would he still enjoy looking at her, touching her? The thoughts hung suspended in her mind as his lips continued to tease and taunt.

"Hunter?" she asked.

He lifted his head.

"Will you still want me when I'm...bigger?"

A moment passed, and then she could feel his blue

eyes scanning her body even in the shadows. "I'll still want you, Eve."

Each time they made love, there were new discoveries, new sounds, new types of caresses, and now as Hunter tasted her body and stroked her skin, she ran her fingers through his hair, loving the feel of it, loving the feel of him. Should she tell him she loved him? Should she ask him if he'd forgiven her refusal of his proposal five years ago?

But just as something kept him guarded, she was afraid to say the words aloud. Sometimes it seemed as if they walked a tightrope, with desire acting as their umbrella and giving them balance. She didn't want to bring up the past when she was hoping they could forget it, and she couldn't tell him of her love until she knew he was ready to believe in love and to believe in her.

So as he gave her pleasure, she gave him pleasure, and afterward she lay by his side wanting to prolong the intimacy between them. But it wasn't long before Hunter shifted away from her and sat up on the edge of the bed. "I'm going to get a drink of water. Would you like anything?"

Sometimes after they made love, he got up and worked. Sometimes he went for a walk. Sometimes he was still awake when she fell asleep. It was as if making love made him restless.

"I'm fine."

Tonight she wasn't asleep when he slipped back into bed. She had the feeling that he wouldn't let himself get close and stay close to her, that it all had something to do with his family. He never wanted to talk about them in any detail. He never wanted to talk about his childhood. Eve remembered what Martha had told her about Larry shutting Hunter out, and from the way he acted now, not much had changed.

"It was good having your family here tonight," she said.

He remained silent.

"Jolene told me she's gotten a promotion."

"She has a good head on her shoulders and she's good with people."

"Midge and Larry's boys got along well with Mark."

"Yes, they did."

"Larry said something to me that puzzled me."

Hunter turned toward her. "What?"

"He said he wished you'd stay out of his affairs."

After a few moments, he asked, "Were you supposed to give me that message?"

"I don't know. I do know he's jealous of you." She'd become certain of that.

"Jealous?" Hunter sounded surprised at the observation. "Larry has no reason to be jealous of me."

Moving closer to her husband, Eve felt her elbow brush his. "That's not true. I think he sees you as the one who made good—out on your own, traveling wherever you want to go, an exciting career."

"*He's* going to be running the family business. What more does he want?" There was a tinge of bitterness in the question.

"Did you want to run the family business?" She knew she might be treading into dangerous territory, but it was time they talked about these things.

"That wasn't in the cards for me."

"But did you want it?" she pressed.

"What I wanted was to be a Morgan, and I wasn't." His clipped tone more than told her this wasn't an area for discussion, and she realized there was a lot of pain underlying his words.

"So why does Larry think you're meddling in his affairs?"

In the ensuing silence she wasn't sure Hunter would answer her. But finally he did. "Because Dad asked me to get him some information, and Larry didn't want to hear what I found."

"John asked for your help?"

"Yes."

"Then he must trust you a lot."

Hunter seemed to mull that over. "Maybe he does."

As they lay there side by side, Eve wondered if John was trying to show Hunter that he and Martha loved him as much as they did Larry and Jolene. Eve laid her hand on top of Hunter's and, although there was still space between them, he intertwined their fingers, and they fell asleep that way.

When Eve awakened the following morning, sun was streaming into the bedroom through the partially open blinds, and she knew she'd overslept. She had to make breakfast. She had to get dressed so she could take Slade and Emily sight-seeing as she'd promised. She had to—

The bedroom door opened and Hunter came in carrying a breakfast tray. He was wearing navy shorts and a white polo shirt and looked as sexy as always. Smiling, he brought the tray over to the bed. There was a red rose in a juice glass, not quite opened.

"What's this?" she asked, all remnants of sleep now gone.

"It's breakfast in bed. Emily and I decided you needed a break."

She looked at the bedside clock. It was ten o'clock. "Why did you let me sleep so late?"

"Because you needed it. Now, I want to see those scrambled eggs and toast disappear." Sitting on the bed, he pushed the tray toward her.

"You expect me to sit here and eat while our company's downstairs?"

His voice was gentle but firm. "Yes, I do. Emily and Slade are going to take Mark sight-seeing today, and I told them we'd watch Amanda."

She took a piece of the toast and had a bite. "You're not going in to work?"

"No. It's their last day here. I'll get caught up tomorrow after I take them to the airport."

"So we're going to watch Amanda?" she asked with a smile.

"Yep. I thought it would be good practice."

"And Emily and Slade trust us?"

"They trust *you*. You've been spending a lot of time with her. But I'll watch and take notes."

His smile and tone made her laugh, and it felt so good to laugh. They needed more laughter between them. "I probably should clean up a little today."

"That's something I wanted to talk to you about."

"You want to help clean?" she asked teasingly.

"Not exactly. Not in the way you mean, anyway. I know you want to continue working while you're pregnant."

"Yes, I do." They'd had this discussion more than once.

"And I know you like to cook."

"I do."

"Then I think you ought to hire a maid service. As you get further along in your pregnancy, you're going to want to use your energy for the things you like to do most, and I don't think cleaning's on that list."

"Unless it's washing the floor with you." She knew she was flirting with him, but it felt so good.

His blue eyes told her he remembered that Saturday vividly. "We can always do that in between when the mood hits," he responded with a grin.

Eve took a few bites of the scrambled eggs. "These are really good. Did you make them?"

"I can't take the credit. They're Emily's. And that rose is from the bush alongside the house that looks like it's growing wild."

Picking up the rose, Eve held it to her nose, inhaling the sweet scent. "It's beautiful, Hunter. Thank you."

"You've made a home here for us, Eve, and I appreciate that." They gazed at each other for a few moments and emotion tightened Eve's throat.

Hunter rose from the bed. "So will you call a maid service?"

"Sure. That will give me a chance to spend more time in the garden."

He shook his head. "We can always hire a gardener for that."

"I love planting and watching things grow. Besides, I've made a new friend. I really like Lauren MacMillan from MacMillan's Garden Center. She can give me lots of tips."

Hunter went to the door. "I'll tell Emily you liked her eggs. Slade said they'll probably leave before you come down. Take your time dressing. Do you think we could take Amanda to the park?"

He looked almost like a kid who was going to start on some great adventure. Because of the number of families in their development, a playground had been erected in a park about three blocks away. "I don't see why not."

Smiling again, he said, "See you downstairs."

"See you downstairs."

She liked the idea of making a playdate with her husband. She liked the idea of getting to know the man behind the exterior he let everyone else see.

Mature trees lined the street that led to the playground. Their home was in a newer part of the development that had grown in stages spanning the past twenty years. As Eve walked beside Hunter over the thick grass leading to the swings and play sets, the sun shone brightly on them. Hunter was wearing sunglasses and as he carried Amanda, every once in a while she reached for them. He laughed, took them off for a while, then put them back on until she reached for them again. It was a game they played on their walk.

They started out on the swings. There were chair seats with safety straps to hold children Amanda's age. She giggled as they took turns pushing her, and she didn't tire of that game for a long while. Afterward, Eve sat with Amanda on the seesaw while Hunter sat on the other end, adjusting his weight so he could bob them up and down. Amanda laughed, and Eve bent down, giving the child a kiss on her cheek. She was so sweet, so precious. Her brown hair was the color of Emily's. Her brown eyes were mischievous and alert and twinkled with a child's innocence.

After a few circles around slowly on the small wooden merry-go-round, Hunter carried Amanda to the shade of an elm. They sat and Eve offered the little girl a zwieback cookie. After she happily took it, she gnawed on it.

"She's going to have another tooth before long," Eve remarked.

"Slade says she grows so fast that he's afraid he'll miss something if he blinks."

"It's hard to believe that at the end of January we'll have a child of our own," Eve murmured, brushing a few crumbs from Amanda's leg.

"I know." Hunter's gaze met hers.

"I just wish I'd been around children more. There's a bookshop near the gallery. I think I'll go to work a little bit early tomorrow and stop in there to pick up a few books on parenting."

"You're a natural." Hunter's voice was low and sincere.

"You are, too. You know, I was thinking. There's no reason we couldn't start decorating the nursery. Even if we don't buy furniture quite yet."

"Are you sure?"

"I'm sure." The silence that settled between them was more comfortable than any she'd ever felt. "What do you want for our son or daughter, Hunter? I mean, what kind of life?"

"I'm not sure what you mean."

"Well, things like schools. I was sent to private schools, but I'm not sure that's always best."

"No, I don't think it is. I'd opt for a good public school, some outside activities but not too many. But most of all, I'd want to teach my son or daughter what's important. I'd want him or her to know we're always here if we're needed. I'd want our child to know there are no ceilings, no barriers, just a wide-open world."

"And what if our son or daughter chooses to be a surfer in L.A.?" she asked.

"Then I hope he or she would be the best darn surfer he or she would know how to be and would have a heck of a lot of fun doing it."

They looked at each other and laughed and then got caught up in the moment, the bright sun, the summer air and being together.

Eve felt lost in the blue of Hunter's eyes until suddenly Amanda decided she didn't want to sit still any longer. Quicker than the breeze, she was on her knees and crawling fast. Hunter scrambled up, but she was a good ten feet away before he caught her.

"Hey, you," he said, scooping her up and tickling her tummy.

She laughed and kicked her feet at him. Almost like a football, he carried her back to where they were sitting and plopped on the ground again with her. "That's scary. She's fast. She could have been in the next county before I knew it."

Eve brushed Amanda's hair from her brow. "I guess you have to keep an eye on them every minute."

"As they get older, and you can't watch them every

minute, then how do you keep them safe?'' Hunter asked.

''You'll find a way,'' she said confidently, knowing that about Hunter.

''*We'll* find a way,'' he responded with a look that made her believe he could forgive her and love her again someday.

Chapter Nine

On Wednesday evening the temperature was a balmy eighty as Eve set the patio table for supper. She missed Slade and Emily and Mark and Amanda. They'd left yesterday morning and the house seemed so empty. Hunter had worked late last night, since he'd taken the morning off to drive Slade and his family to the airport. So tonight Eve was looking forward to some quiet time alone with him. A FedEx package had come for him earlier and she'd laid it on the glass table next to his place so she wouldn't forget to give it to him. She was setting salads on the table on the patio when she heard him pull into the garage. A few minutes later he came outside.

"Hi," she said with a smile. "How was your day?"

"Busy. How about yours?"

"I sold two paintings this morning," she said proudly. "And the woman's bringing her husband in tomorrow morning to consult on a sculpture."

"You should be working on commission," Hunter teased, then he spied the package by his place setting.

She handed it to him. "This came about an hour ago."

He opened it quickly and took out a computer disk and a sheaf of papers. After he analyzed them a few moments, he said, "I thought so."

"What?" Eve asked.

"It's the proof I need to show Larry once and for all that the merger he's planning could sink Morgan's Office Products permanently."

"What kind of proof?"

"I have a friend who's a security consultant and is good with databases and the like. I have financial documents here that prove the company that Larry wants to merge with has been doing some creative bookkeeping. They're reporting revenues they don't have. It's what my father suspected."

"Do you think Larry will listen to you?"

"He has no choice. The information's here in black and white."

Just then the doorbell chimes rang. They could be heard even out on the patio.

"I'll get it," Eve offered.

When she opened the front door, she found Barbara Kellogg, the woman who had been so familiar with Hunter at the cocktail party Eve had attended. She was smiling and dressed in a navy summer business suit with white high heels. The suit showed off her curves, and Eve considered the hem of her skirt much too short for the office. Besides her purse, she held a manila envelope.

"Hello," Eve said politely, wishing she could close

the door and tell the woman Hunter was nowhere around.

"Hi. I have some papers for Hunter."

This woman had more than papers for Hunter, Eve guessed, but she supposed she had no recourse but to let her inside. She wished she'd had a chance to change before Hunter came home. Her mint-green, terry culotte outfit and white sandals made her feel underdressed.

Before she had a chance to invite Barbara inside, Hunter came into the foyer. "Barbara." He sounded surprised.

"Hi, Hunter. You said you needed these figures as soon as I had them ready."

"I don't think that little French perfume company you want to buy will sell out to anyone else until they get your offer."

"You know once I get an idea I like to move on it," Barbara said in that intimate kind of tone that told Eve she and Hunter had had many dealings before. "Besides. You told me about your new house and offered to give me a personal tour. Here I am."

Hunter took the envelope from her. "The tour starts here. Come on. I'll show you around."

The last thing Eve was going to do was trail along. "I'll make sure supper doesn't burn," she said sweetly as she went to the kitchen.

Hunter just arched a brow, but beckoned Barbara into the family room. "We spend a lot of our time in here."

When Barbara crossed over to the fireplace, Eve went to the kitchen. She could hear Barbara exclaiming about the merits of vaulted ceilings.

Eve turned down the oven and then heard Barbara's high heels on the steps. They were going upstairs. She'd probably asked for a private tour of the master bedroom. That woman had gall, Eve would give her that.

Although Eve busied herself in the kitchen, she was aware of time passing, much too much of it. But finally Hunter and Barbara came downstairs again and disappeared into the living room, and then to the room beyond that held Emory Ruskin's paintings. Eve knew she had to stop thinking about the art that way. They were Hunter's now. She'd signed them over.

She didn't regret it, but every now and then she remembered that the title of the house was in his name only. Not that she cared about owning half the house. But if Hunter had trusted her...

Eve was putting dollops of whipped cream on a strawberry pie when Hunter and Barbara came into the kitchen.

"Nice work space," Barbara commented. "But I never have time to cook." She looked over at Eve and the pie. "You must spend a lot of your time in here."

The way Barbara said it, it sounded as if Eve had no other interests and her life work was cooking. "Some," Eve said. "I enjoy it. Along with gardening and working at the art gallery."

"You work?" Barbara asked with a raised brow.

"Yes. I have a degree in art history."

"I see. So you're the creative type."

Again, it sounded more like an insult than a compliment and Eve wondered how Barbara and Larry would get along together, although she didn't think Barbara's cattiness came from insecurity. Eve would bet she was just trying to make some kind of point with Hunter.

Eve's upbringing and a desire to show Hunter she could be gracious led her to ask, "Would you like to stay for supper?"

"What a lovely idea. But I can't. I have another meeting tonight. Hunter knows all about those. We went to almost ten last night, didn't we?"

So Hunter's meeting had been with Barbara last night?

Eve had the most ridiculous desire to throw the strawberry pie straight at the woman, but she never had been a woman of impulse. Propriety usually led her to say and do the right thing. There were books of wallpaper samples lying on the floor of the room that was going to be the nursery. Eve wondered if Hunter had told Barbara they were expecting.

"It's really a shame you can't stay for supper," Eve remarked, sure she could manage to spill something on Barbara in the course of a meal. Her father had always told her to get to know her enemies. And though she'd never had any, Barbara sure fit the bill.

The blonde took a quick glance at her watch. "I'd better get going." She laid her hand familiarly on Hunter's elbow. "Thanks so much for the tour."

"I'll walk you out," he said.

Temptation almost convinced Eve to peek into the foyer while they said goodbye, but she didn't. Instead she took the roast out of the oven and made a lot of noise doing it.

A few minutes later, Hunter came back to the kitchen and, with arms crossed, leaned against the doorjamb, watching Eve as she transferred the roast to a platter and took the electric knife from a drawer.

"That was unexpected," he said.

"Was it?" She couldn't keep the pique out of her question.

"Say what you have to say, Eve."

"You invited her here."

He gave a sort of half shrug. "It wasn't exactly an invitation. We were making conversation last night, and I told her about the house."

"And you asked her to come over?"

"She said she'd like to see it sometime, and I told her to stop by. But I really didn't expect her to."

"Then you must have your head buried in the sand," Eve muttered.

Uncrossing his arms, Hunter pushed away from the doorjamb, came over to the counter and stood very close to her. "And that means?"

The masculine power that emanated from Hunter had once intimidated Eve. Now, instead, it intrigued her and excited her and at the moment made her angry. "That means she wants to take up wherever the two of you left off."

"There was nothing there to continue." His voice was even and patient, as if he were explaining to a child.

His tone added fuel to her simmering anger. "Sex means something different to most women than it does to men. Maybe she expected more than a good time."

"She knew the score, and I certainly never made any promises."

"She's the type of woman who doesn't give up easily," Eve insisted. "She still wants you."

"I'm married to you now," he responded soberly.

His answer wasn't enough. She wanted more, and she pushed for it. "Did you tell her I'm expecting?"

"No."

"Why not?"

When he moved even closer to her, she found her back against the counter. "Are you accusing me of something?" he asked.

"Are you still attracted to her?" Eve countered, not backing down.

"I told you before. She's my client now, Eve. That's all she is."

"Your other clients don't turn up at our home at suppertime," Eve flared, not at all satisfied, needing to know just how important she was to her husband.

"Why does that bother you so?" he asked, his expression undecipherable.

She couldn't keep the truth sugarcoated. "Because I don't appreciate having your former girlfriends parade through our home."

Blowing out an exasperated breath, he leaned away. "What did you want me to do? I didn't want to be rude. You're making too much of this. You can't get uptight every time I run into somebody I dated."

She could have screamed with frustration at not being able to break through his barriers, at not being able to find out what he really felt about her. "Just how many women *have* you dated, Hunter? Will I be running into one every few months, or maybe every few weeks?"

"Are you asking me how many women I've slept with since you?"

Faced with that blunt question, she felt her throat

tighten with quick tears, and she shook her head. "Never mind. I don't want to know."

Instead of towering over her, he braced a hand on either side of her against the counter. "Maybe I want to know how many men *you've* slept with." The deep blue of his eyes told her he wouldn't back down from this, and that this moment could be an important one in their marriage.

"There haven't been any other men. Only you."

He looked startled. "You expect me to believe that?"

"Yes. The same way you expect me to believe that you weren't involved with anyone after you left Savannah."

The silence in the kitchen was so loud it vibrated.

Abruptly Hunter stepped back. "We'd better eat before supper gets cold."

The companionship and connection she'd felt with him the past few days dissolved. Their past had sprung up between them again.

Eve wasn't the least bit hungry. Barbara's visit had unsettled her, and it was obvious that her answer to Hunter's question wasn't one he could believe. Supper was awkward, and after a few stilted attempts at conversation, they gave up trying.

Hunter glanced over at his wife often throughout the meal. He'd been surprised by her reaction to Barbara.

Last night, during their meeting, his client had let him know in very subtle ways that she was available if he still wanted to see her. Apparently she didn't give marriage vows a lot of weight. But he did. He'd seen his mom and dad's marriage and what it had meant to them both. There had never been any doubt of fidelity or commitment.

When Eve had begun questioning him, he'd felt defensive—as if he had to try to justify putting her out of his life five years ago, trying to get her out of his mind. He'd never expected her response to his question, and he still didn't know if he believed it. She was a beautiful woman with so much passion to give. Had she really bottled that up? Turned inward? Had the miscarriage affected her that much?

The past week or so, he'd found things changing between them. He'd been a little less cautious, talking more easily about what was important to him. But what would happen if he threw caution to the wind? What would happen if Eve turned away from him? If she decided she didn't need him anymore?

That night five years ago when they'd made love had been life-changing for him. He'd thought he'd found someone who could look into his soul and care for him more deeply than anyone had ever cared about him. Then he'd asked her to marry him and she'd refused. He'd never wanted to admit it, but it had been a devastating blow.

Looking at her now as she toyed with the piece of strawberry pie, he realized he needed some time to think. He needed some space between them, so he didn't pull her into his arms. He had plenty of work to do at the office. It had always been a refuge, and tonight that's what he needed.

Pushing back his chair, he said, "I'm going back to the office tonight."

"All right." She sounded as if she'd expected it. "Hunter, about Barbara."

"I think she's taken up enough of our time tonight." He stood. "But if you want me to drop her as a client, I will."

Eve looked up at him, studying him carefully. If she accepted his offer, he'd know she didn't trust him, he'd know that this marriage they were trying to build was even shakier than he thought.

"No, don't drop her. If you say whatever you had with her is finished, then I believe you."

Relief washed over him, and he couldn't help but caress Eve's cheek, take her chin in his hand, bend down to kiss her. As always, their passion was hot and fiery. But tonight he needed some space more than he needed passion.

Yet he couldn't help but murmur, "You're the only woman I want, Eve," before he straightened and went into the kitchen.

The next morning at the Sandstone Gallery, Eve unwrapped a painting by a new artist, which had been shipped in from North Carolina. Usually she loved unwrapping each new piece, discovering an artist all for herself. But today she was distracted by what had happened between her and Hunter last night. She just couldn't figure out what was going on in his head. When he'd kissed her so fiercely, then told her he wanted only her, she'd felt so happy, yet so unsettled, too. Because he was leaving...because he obviously needed space between them.

He'd even left the disk and printouts—which had seemed so important to him—on the patio chair. She'd put them safely on the desk in his office and had hoped she'd still be awake when he came in. But with her pregnancy, fatigue often made her eyes close before she wanted them to.

In the middle of the night she remembered feeling his body beside her. Once, she'd snuggled close to him, but he'd been asleep. When she'd awakened this morning, he was already gone.

The security buzzer on the gallery's door sounded as a customer came in. Setting the painting she'd unwrapped on an easel, she crossed to the counter and desk. When she recognized the customer, she was surprised. It was Larry Morgan. As far as she knew from their computer listing of customers, he'd never bought anything at the Sandstone Gallery. But that didn't mean he didn't look on occasion, she supposed.

"Hi, Larry. Can I help you with something?" she asked.

"I was in the area on an errand and thought I'd stop in to see if you were here."

"As you can see, I am," she said with a smile, reminding herself he was Hunter's brother, reminding herself that he might not have an ax to grind. Yet her intuition told her otherwise.

"Midge was impressed with those paintings in that special room you have. She said we should think about investing in something like that. So I thought this might be a good place to start."

They had a variety of styles, techniques and forms. "Do you have any idea of what you'd like?"

"I'll know it when I see it."

Lots of customers shopped that way—the perfect painting for the perfect spot—but she had a feeling Larry wasn't one of them. "Midge told me she particularly liked the Wyeth."

Larry looked blank. "Actually, I think I'd prefer a seascape."

"Watercolor or oil?"

He gave a nonchalant shrug. "It doesn't matter."

"Over here." She beckoned him to follow as she crossed to a corner of the gallery where two watercolors hung.

Larry peered at the price. "You think you'd get more for your money," he muttered.

"I have large prints that you can have framed. Some of them are signed limited editions."

He shook his head. "I'll just wander around. Don't mind me."

"All right. Just let me know if you need help." Eve returned to the desk near the counter to finish cataloging the painting she'd unwrapped. As she recorded information into the computer, she was aware of Larry wandering about. Finally he came over to the desk.

"I might wait till closer to the holidays, then buy something for Midge for Christmas."

"That would be a lovely gift. She'd have something to treasure always."

"I guess women like that idea."

Larry didn't seem in any hurry to leave and she suspected now she'd learn the real reason for his visit.

Absently, he looked through a brochure on the counter. "So...has Hunter given up the idea of trying to interfere in my business?"

She wouldn't lie. "I don't think he sees it as interfering, Larry. You'll probably be hearing from him soon."

"Why?" Hunter's brother asked, his eyes narrowed. "What's he going to do now?"

"This really isn't any of my business."

"I'm making it your business. You're Hunter's wife. What's he planning?"

She just shook her head. "He's not planning anything. He found out some information that might help all of you, that's all."

"That's all," Larry mumbled. "I bet. You don't know what kind of information?"

"You really ought to talk to Hunter about this. Call him, Larry. Ask him."

"I have some other people to call first." With that, he left the brochure open on the counter, turned and exited the shop.

Eve left the gallery around two, drove home and opened all the windows to the fresh summer air, wondering if she should tell Hunter about Larry's visit. She didn't want to stir up trouble between them. As she tried to decide whether Hunter would prefer hamburgers on the grill or a meat loaf, the phone rang. She picked it up.

"Mrs. Coleburn, this is Sandra Grayson."

"Yes, Sandra. You're still coming tomorrow morning to clean?" Eve had gotten Sandra's name from a reputable employment service Hunter had recommended. She was married, the mother of two, and cleaned houses to put money away for her children's college fund.

"That's why I'm calling. My little girl is sick. Nothing serious, just a cold. But my husband will be here tonight and I might have to take her to the doctor's tomorrow. So I wondered if it would be okay with you if I came over this evening and cleaned?"

Hesitating only a few moments—she didn't even know if Hunter would be home for supper or if he'd be working late—she answered, "Sure, that's no problem."

"Is it all right if I come over around four?"

"That's fine. There won't be much to do this time, just sweeping and dusting."

"Thank you. I really appreciate this. I'll see you then."

Eve hung up and then called Hunter to see what his plans were. Maybe they could just go out for dinner. The receptionist told Eve that Hunter was out of the office but that she expected him back any time and she'd give him the message. An hour later Eve tried Hunter's cell phone. But he didn't answer, and she guessed he'd left it in his car. She didn't want to page him simply to discuss dinner plans.

Hunter hadn't returned Eve's message by the time Sandra arrived. Eve decided that when he came home, she'd convince him they needed a dinner by candlelight someplace quiet. She showed Sandra what she wanted her to do and how to operate the central vacuum. Then Sandra told Eve she'd start with the bedrooms. The young mother had brought a carrier with her own supplies, was efficient and thoroughly capable. Eve left her to do her work and went downstairs.

After she settled on the patio with a glass of lemonade and directions for knitting baby booties, she heard Hunter's footsteps coming through the kitchen. Startled, she looked up. She hadn't even heard the garage door open. As he usually did for work, he was wearing a white shirt, but the sleeves were rolled up, his tie tugged down. He was holding the computer disk and papers that had arrived yesterday, and he looked upset.

"I didn't even hear the garage door."

"I parked in the driveway and came in the front. I'll be leaving again. Who's the van belong to?"

"The lady who's cleaning for us. She's upstairs. What's wrong, Hunter? You look upset."

"Upset? That's an understatement." He rubbed the back of his neck. "Dad called me. He just found out that Larry moved up the plans to sign the final papers for the merger. They're meeting in Farley's lawyer's office at six o'clock. I told Dad to call Jolene and get her over there, and I'd meet them with the information Simon sent me. I don't know why Larry decided to do this now instead of waiting until September."

Eve knew, and she suddenly felt sick to her stomach. "I think I know why."

"How would you know?" Hunter's question was like a shot from a cannon, almost accusatory.

"Larry came into the gallery today. At first he acted as if he were interested in buying a painting or a sculpture, but then he asked me if you were planning to interfere in his business plans any further."

"And what did you say?"

"I told him that you'd gotten some information—"

Eve had never seen Hunter look as angry as he did at that moment. He exploded. "I told you what I did in confidence! You should have kept it to yourself."

"But I didn't really tell him anything."

"You told him enough, apparently. He didn't set up this meeting because the sky was blue today." Hunter's usual lawyer's calm was gone, and she saw the fury in his blue eyes.

"I was only trying to help you work things out."

"Your *help* could cost my family their business. Besides that, you betrayed my confidence. When will I learn that I can't trust you, Eve?"

Hunter's feelings were finally out in the open, and now that they were, she didn't know what to do or say. "You can trust me, Hunter."

"No, I can't. Five years ago, I thought we meant something to each other. You gave the impression that what I was feeling wasn't one-sided, that you were involved as much as I was. When I kissed you, you kissed me back like there was no tomorrow. And when we made love—" He shook his head. "When we made love, I gave you everything I was, Eve. But you tossed aside what I had to give. Your dad as much as told me I wasn't good enough for you, that he had plans for you. I thought what you felt would guide you more than his rules or his strategies or his need to have you marry the right man."

"Hunter, I was young. I—"

"Yes, you were young," he cut in. "But you were old enough to know exactly what you were doing. With a face and body like yours along with all of that Southern charm, you knew how to wrap a man around your finger. I let you do it because I was searching for something more than I'd ever found, because I was searching for some kind of bond that would last a lifetime."

"Hunter, I'm sorry."

His expression was more grim than she'd ever seen it, and his voice was condemning. "You're sorry. You're sorry about refusing my marriage proposal. You're sorry you didn't tell me about your pregnancy.

You're sorry about your miscarriage and the fact you never told me about that, either. And now you're sorry about something that was supposed to be between the two of us but you decided to reveal to my brother. *I'm sorry* just doesn't cut it, Eve. If I can't stop this merger—'' He sucked in a deep breath. ''I don't have time for this now. I've got to get across town.''

She reached out to him. ''Please, Hunter, you have to listen to me—''

''No, Eve, I don't. I'm beginning to doubt that I should have ever considered your marriage proposal.''

Each and every one of his words had hurt her so deeply she couldn't find her voice. When she did, he was already gone.

Chapter Ten

When Eve heard the front door close, she almost ran after Hunter. But what good would that do? He obviously didn't trust her. He'd obviously never forgiven her. What kind of marriage could they have with that resentment always between them?

It wouldn't do any good to tell herself she'd been trying to help with Larry. If only he and Hunter could find some common ground. If only Larry could forget his insecurity and jealousy, then Hunter could reach outside his isolation. But now...

Whether the merger went through or not, Hunter would not likely forgive her breach of confidence. And whether she'd meant it to be that or not, that's what it was.

Hunter would never believe it now if she told him she loved him. She did love him—with all of her heart and soul. What would happen if they couldn't get past this? What would happen if he closed himself off from her forever?

Tears came to her eyes and she couldn't blink them away. They ran down her cheeks for a long time, and she didn't know what to think or what to do. If she waited here for Hunter—

She had no idea when he'd be back. She had no idea *if* he'd be back.

When the phone rang, her heart skipped a beat. Maybe it was Hunter. Maybe he *could* understand. But when she picked it up, she heard "It's Lauren, Eve."

"Oh. Hi, Lauren."

"Is something wrong?"

She liked Lauren, but she didn't know her that well yet. So she said, "I've had an unusual day."

"Well, I'm hoping not to make it too unusual. I have the plans finished for your gardens. Would you like to see them?"

"Tonight?"

"I'm free, if you are. Actually, you said you were often alone in the evenings. I'm in Denver with another client right now, but if you'd like to drive in, we could go somewhere for dinner."

She was too upset to eat, but she had to eat for the baby's sake. Sitting here feeling sorry for herself certainly wasn't going to help her. Maybe she could get some perspective if she had dinner with Lauren. Maybe she could think of a way to show Hunter how much she loved him. Maybe she could find a way to make him understand why she'd refused him five years ago, but why she'd asked him to marry her now.

"Where would you like to meet?" she asked Lauren.

Hunter's dad had told him where the meeting was supposed to be held—at the law offices of a firm that was considered less than reputable. That in itself should have been a clear signal to Larry that something wasn't on the up-and-up. But Larry was trying so hard to prove something to himself, and maybe to Hunter, that he couldn't see beyond his nose.

As Hunter parked his car and went to the door of the office building, he saw the blue sky had turned gray. That sure fit his mood. So did the stormy clouds and the wind picking up. His gut was burning with the bitter taste of Eve's breach of trust—just another in a long line, as far as he was concerned. He purposefully pushed thoughts of Eve away as he went inside.

He found everyone gathered in a reception area, and noticed John's relieved look when he saw Hunter. "There you are. I told them we weren't going into that room and signing anything until you got here."

Otis Farley was a hefty man, about six feet tall, with a suit coat that barely covered his midriff. "I don't see what his arrival has to do with this, Morgan. All the parties concerned are already here."

His face flushed with anger, Larry stood. "I don't know what this is all about. Hunter, you can just turn around and leave. We don't need you here."

But Jolene clasped Larry's elbow. "Larry, please listen to Hunter. Just see what he has with him."

"The infamous information Eve spoke about. I'm surprised you didn't bring her along, too."

Hunter's heart hurt, but he ignored it. "Larry, all I ask is that you listen to me for five minutes. That's all. And take a look at these papers."

John came over and clasped Larry on the shoulder.

"Please, son. Just listen to what your brother has to say."

Startled, Hunter looked at his father. John Morgan was speaking as if both sons were equals, as if he looked at each of them the same way.

Still looking disgruntled, staring first at his father and then at Jolene and then finally at Hunter, Larry said, "All right. Five minutes. Let's step out into the hall."

Larry, Jolene, Hunter and John went out into the hall while Farley and his lawyer stayed behind.

"This had better be good," Larry muttered. "You're making me look like a fool."

Without comment, Hunter handed Larry the pages documenting information on the disk. "These are Farley's balance sheets. They're supposed to be a matter of public record, but they weren't easy to get. I have a friend who managed it for me. You can take the time to study them, but basically what you'll find is what's called an inappropriate recognition of revenue. In other words, Farley is putting money on the books that his company doesn't have. And he's being investigated for it."

Larry quickly looked over the papers—the numbers and the columns. Then he paled and looked up at Hunter. "This is serious."

"Yes, it's serious. You sign papers for a merger with this company, and you're putting Morgan's Office Products in jeopardy." That was the bottom line and there was no way he could make it easy to swallow.

Silence reverberated in the hallway until a door slammed shut somewhere in the building. Hunter didn't know what to expect from Larry, and he prepared himself for anything, including more accusations that he was trying to ruin the deal for his own reasons.

"Why did you do this?" Larry asked.

"I didn't do it to ruin the deal."

"Why *did* you do it?"

"I told you before. Dad felt uncomfortable about Farley. He'd heard rumors, and he asked me to look into them."

"I should have researched Farley more thoroughly myself," Larry murmured.

Jolene said gently, "You wouldn't listen to Dad. You were so sure this was the right thing to do."

Larry glanced at Hunter. "No, not the right thing to do. It was the thing that would put me in *his* league. All of these years I've been trying to be self-confident, as sure of myself, as good at handling Morgan's as Hunter is with his law practice. And now I almost brought down the whole company."

To his sons John said, "There's no reason for you two to compete. You are both my sons. You always have been and you always will be. I don't have a favorite, though neither of you believes that. Your mother doesn't have a favorite. Hunter, you aren't less of a son because you were adopted. We chose you. And Larry, you're not less of a son because Hunter's older and came first. I thought we tried to make that clear to both of you over the years, but we never succeeded."

Hunter heard the sincerity in his father's voice. His dad had come to him for help and had trusted and respected his opinion...so much so that John Morgan had stopped this merger meeting without having absolute proof in his hands.

Jolene stepped to Hunter's side. "We never knew each other very well. I always felt if I tried to get close to you, I was being disloyal to Larry somehow. That wasn't fair to any of us. But I think of you as my brother, Hunter, just as I do Larry."

Hunter's chest tightened.

Jolene said to her father and Larry, "Why don't you go inside and tell Mr. Farley the deal is off."

Still looking shaken, Larry glanced at John and then nodded. He put his hand on the doorknob, but before he turned it, he looked at Hunter. "Thanks."

At that moment, Hunter didn't know if he and Larry would be close, but he did know that somehow they'd made a start. Today wasn't one he'd soon forget.

After John and Larry went inside, Jolene faced Hunter. "You know, don't you, that it wasn't Mom and Dad's fault that you felt adopted. It was more of Larry's and mine."

"I've never seen all of it with much objectivity," Hunter admitted.

"Did you know that after your accident, Mom and Dad never left your side, except when Slade or I were with you?"

"No."

"I didn't think so. Those days when you were in a coma were the worst days Mom and Dad ever spent. They sat by your bed, and talked to you, and cried and prayed. They love you, Hunter, every bit as much as they love Larry and me."

Hunter couldn't speak for a few moments. "I've

been so foolish blaming them for leaving Slade behind.''

"I've heard them talking about it since Slade found you. They've felt guilt over the years, Hunter. Guilt that they separated you from your twin. But they had to make decisions, and as people say—hindsight is twenty-twenty.''

"I've always known you were smart. I just didn't know you were wise, too.'' Suddenly he felt as if he really did have a sister.

"Not so wise. I'm just not in the middle of it like you are.'' She gave Hunter a smile. "You know, Larry might be easier to live with now, if you don't lord this over him.''

Hunter smiled back. "I wouldn't do that.''

"He kept complaining to me before you got here that Eve should have told him what this information was. But deep down, I think he admired her being loyal to you. And if he'd taken her advice and talked to you about it, this never would have happened.''

"Eve told him to talk to me about it?''

"Yes. I think Larry likes her, even though he won't come right out and say it. Must be that Southern accent.''

Larry liked Eve. Eve had been loyal. Hunter's whole world felt as if it had turned upside down. He'd accused her of betraying his confidence. He'd accused her...

The door opened, and Larry and John Morgan stepped out into the hall again. "We're finished with Farley,'' Larry said. "And I've changed my mind about merging. I'd probably have to give up too much control.'' He glanced up at Hunter. "And that's hard for me.''

"It's hard for anyone,'' Hunter agreed.

"Why don't we all go out for dinner?'' Larry suggested. "We can toast our nonmerger.''

Everyone laughed. Part of Hunter felt light, but the other part felt very heavy when he thought of Eve and the things he'd said to her. "I'd really like to come to dinner with you, but what if I join you for a drink instead? I need to get home tonight.''

"I suppose you still are a newlywed,'' Larry gibed.

Hunter could look at Larry in a new light now. Eve had been right about him, too. Insecurity had always driven him and made him cut Hunter out. Now maybe they could start being brothers.

And maybe, after he shared a drink with his brother, sister and father, he could figure out what to do about Eve.

An hour later, Hunter arrived home. The storm clouds had opened and rain was pouring down in driving sheets. The van was still sitting in the driveway. He opened the garage door and pulled in, then switched off the ignition. Eve's car was gone. He suddenly felt panic as he'd never felt before. *Where* had she gone?

Had she left the house? Or had she left his life?

Following the hall into the kitchen, he found a note on the island, but he didn't experience any relief until he read it.

Hunter,
    Lauren MacMillan finished her plans for our

gardens. I've gone to dinner with her to discuss them. I won't be late.

                                        Eve

Our gardens?

She'd worked so hard turning this house into a home, even after he'd put the title only in his name. That didn't seem to matter to her. He'd been afraid to admit how much he liked sharing his life with her, how he couldn't wait to see her every night, how he was counting the days until their baby would be born.

Somehow they'd make things right tonight.

He heard the noise in the family room. As he went through, he saw a brunette in her twenties, dressed in jeans and a T-shirt, running the vacuum cleaner. She turned it off and smiled at him.

"Hi. You must be Mr. Coleburn. I'm Sandra Grayson. I should be finished in about half an hour."

"Do you know what time my wife left?"

"I think it was around seven."

Hunter glanced at the rain streaming down the windows. It was almost dark, and he didn't like the idea of Eve being out in the rainstorm. Sometimes there was flash flooding....

"I'm going to get a quick shower. If the phone rings, will you answer it? It might be Eve stranded somewhere."

"Sure. I'll do that."

A trace of a memory flickered in his mind. As he went to the stairs, he suddenly stopped. Déjà vu. He'd been staying in a hotel in Florence, Italy. The maid had come in to turn down his bed. Expecting a business call, he'd said to her, "Will you answer the phone if it rings?"

She'd nodded, and he'd gone into the shower.

That had been about six weeks after he'd left Savannah, Georgia. He remembered because he'd walked the streets of Florence that day, knowing how much Eve would have enjoyed it—the art, the statues, the buildings.

What if that had been the night Eve had called? What if the woman she'd talked to had been a maid?

He hadn't believed her, and he'd been keeping her at arm's length because of it…and so much more.

Hunter showered, letting the water sluice over him, trying to absorb everything that had happened today, everything that had happened in his life.

When had he started distrusting? When his parents had died and he and Slade were placed at the boys' home? He hadn't even been aware of it as a baby, but maybe something down deep inside him had. Maybe something down deep inside had told him that the people who cared for him weren't really connected to him. Then he'd been adopted, and Slade had been left behind. He'd been too young to realize he'd been separated from his twin, but some part of him had known. He'd been alone; he'd always felt alone…ever since he could remember feeling.

John and Martha Morgan had adopted him, and he was sure they'd cared for him and loved him. But their lives had been in turmoil—a new job, a new town and then another new baby. Larry's jealousy must have started early.

And he'd felt alone.

That aloneness had persisted until he'd met Eve. Five years ago, she'd seemed to be the piece of his heart that had been missing. He'd known it instantly.

He'd known it dramatically. He'd known it confidently.

How overpowering and terrifying that must have been for a nineteen-year-old girl to find herself the center of an older man's attention...attraction...desire. She'd been sheltered. She'd been inexperienced. And if she'd had feelings similar to his, they probably went deeper than anything she'd ever felt before.

All these years he'd been bitter about her refusal, angry because she'd turned him away. He hadn't been angry with just her; he'd been angry with fate...for that aloneness. *And* at Eve because she could have eased it. Since then he'd been living his life automatically, taking pleasure and satisfaction where he could, not feeling real joy. Not until Slade had found him. Slade had made a difference that Hunter only now realized. But even with their reunion, there'd been bitterness against his parents for separating him from his twin.

Rumbles of thunder penetrated Hunter's soul-searching, and he quickly finished in the shower and got out, drying himself off, barely aware of pulling khaki shorts and a white T-shirt from a drawer. Slipping on moccasins, he went downstairs. Sandra was putting cleaning supplies back in her carrier. He paid her, and then asked, "Are you sure you want to leave in this?"

"I don't have far to go. I'll be fine."

Hunter watched her run to her van, start it up and pull out of the driveway. Then he switched on the weather channel and was dismayed by what he saw. The storms in the area were causing flash flooding.

His heart raced faster as he worried about Eve being out in the storm.

What if something happened to her?

To *her,* not just to their baby.

She'd become his life. She'd become his...

Love.

He'd been afraid to see it, afraid to admit it, afraid to say it.

When she came home, he'd tell her what an idiot he'd been. He'd apologize to her. He'd ask her to truly be his wife.

When she came home.

Rain splashed down the plate-glass windows of the restaurant where Eve sat with Lauren at dinner. She was looking over the plans Lauren had drawn up for the gardens, but she couldn't keep her mind on them. She couldn't keep her mind on anything. Believing that coming out to dinner tonight would help sort her thoughts had been a mistake.

Lauren was saying, "So if you like the flat slate rocks, we could use those, or... Eve, are you all right?"

Eve looked up. From the time she'd spent with Lauren, she knew the landscape architect was perceptive and would recognize a denial if she heard one. She shook her head as tears came to her eyes.

"What's wrong? Is it the pregnancy?"

Eve shook her head again. Her problems with Hunter were private, and she believed she should keep them that way.

"Is it your husband?" Lauren probed, sincerely concerned, not just curious.

"We're having some problems. It's complicated and I…I really can't talk about it."

Lauren's brown eyes studied her. "You're not afraid of him, are you?"

"Oh, no. I'm not afraid of Hunter. I could never be afraid of him."

Lauren looked relieved. "And you love him?"

Tears fell down Eve's cheeks. "So much that he's become my world."

Lauren leaned forward slightly, her eyes sparkling. "I've seen my parents love each other through ups and downs and ins and outs. They've been married for the past thirty-five years. I don't think there's any problem that love can't fix."

Eve hadn't been around very many marriages to know that. But she wanted to believe it. "I'm hoping you're right. And I've got to get home. The plans are great. They really are."

"Why don't you wait until the storm lets up a little?"

Eve shook her head. "I can't wait. If Hunter is there…I have to talk to him." She opened her purse to take her share of the bill from it.

"Supper's on me," Lauren said with a smile.

"I insist." Eve started to protest.

Lauren grinned. "You can't insist. You can pay next time. And please, be careful driving."

Her friendship with Lauren had sprung up so quickly, but Eve knew it was the kind that lasted. After she rolled up the plans and said goodbye, she dashed to her car. Water was already brimming over the curb.

Her drive home was tedious. Some streets were flooded, and she had to take detours. She drove slowly, watching her speed, careful the pools of water didn't throw her car. The drive took twice as long as it should have, and when she pushed her remote to open the garage door, her hands were shaking. But she saw Hunter's car inside.

She lowered the door again, then went through the hall to the kitchen. Hunter was standing at the sink, and his expression was... She wasn't sure what it was.

"Eve," he breathed. "I was so worried. I called the gallery, thinking you might have stopped there after dinner. But nobody answered. Then I called the police, but the reported accidents didn't involve your car." He stopped suddenly and just stared at her.

"I'm sorry you worried...." Her voice caught. He must still have feelings for her.

"I was *more* than worried. I was afraid maybe you wouldn't come back."

"Where would I go?" she asked quietly.

"Any place I'm not. I've been such an absolute jackass. Tonight I remembered something and— There was a maid in my room that night in Florence, Eve. There wasn't another woman. She'd come in to turn the covers back. I'd gone into the shower. I'm so sorry I didn't get your call. I'm so sorry I didn't believe you'd tried. I've been blind. There've been so many things clouding how I felt, how I *feel*. I love you, Eve. I've always loved you. You. Not just the idea of having a baby with you. Not just the idea of having a family with you. But you."

Eve couldn't believe what she saw in Hunter's eyes. She couldn't believe the words she was hearing. And he must have seen that disbelief on her face.

Crossing to her, he took her purse and the rolled-up plans from her hand and laid them on the island. "Can you forgive me for blaming you for everything that happened? For my bitterness? For not loving you the way you should be loved?"

Tears ran down Eve's cheeks. "Can you forgive me for being afraid of love the first time I felt it? For not trying hard enough to reach you? I loved you then, Hunter. I was just so afraid."

He gently laid his fingertips over her lips. But then his thumb trailed across her cheek. "What about now, Eve? What do you feel now?"

The urgency in his voice told her she had to open her heart completely. "I feel so much it still scares me. There's never been anyone but you, Hunter. And I think my father knew that. That's why he put that clause in his will, hoping it would lead me to happiness. I didn't come to you to propose to you simply to get my inheritance. I knew it was the one chance I had to make my dreams come true. Because you've always filled my dreams, as well as my heart."

"Oh, Eve," Hunter breathed as he bent his head and possessively claimed her lips.

She surrendered completely as she gave him her love, and he gave her his. He broke away once, but as she reached her arms up around his neck, he came back to her again as if kissing her and holding her was the only thing in this world that mattered. She melded against him, settling her body against his, and he groaned, sweeping her mouth with his tongue, caressing her back, holding her with such a sense of longing she didn't want him to ever let her go.

Suddenly he broke away and held her face between his hands. "So you can forgive me?"

"Yes. And you can forgive me?"

"Anything."

Then she wondered what had happened to his family's business. "What happened at the meeting?"

"You won't believe everything that went on at that meeting—before and after it." Without warning, he swept her up into his arms to carry her upstairs. "Everything's fine. I'll tell you all about it. Later."

Eve thought she'd felt desire for Hunter before, and that he'd felt it for her. But nothing had prepared her for their hearts and bodies coming together in a complete union of love. Their naked bodies were a means of communication that went beyond words, and sighs, and thoughts, and touch. Hunter's touches had never been so tender. His eyes filled with so much emotion that it poured into her. She embraced him with a freedom she'd never felt before.

They gave each other their hearts and souls and bodies, with vulnerability and passion and all-consuming love. When Hunter entered her, she clung to him, knowing there were no barriers between them and no past regrets. As they reached the height of fulfillment at the same moment, their future burst before them, almost overwhelming in its glorious intensity.

Afterward, they stayed joined together, lying on their sides, still touching and kissing and appreciating.

Hunter kissed her temple. "I've missed so much, Eve. Not only with you, but with my family."

She heard the guilt in his voice, and she stroked his jaw, waiting for him to go on.

"I'm still trying to let it all sink in. But my parents have always loved me as much as Larry and Jolene. Circumstances just made me unable to accept it. Larry listened to me today, and I listened to my dad and Jolene. Maybe none of us had ever really listened to each other before. I don't know. But I think everything is going to be different now."

"Different? How?"

"Closer. Jolene told me how my mom and dad never left my side when I was in the coma, how they cried and prayed and talked to me. When I woke up, Slade was there, and they weren't. And I'd thought… Well…it doesn't matter what I'd thought. I was wrong—about that and about so many other things."

She wrapped her arm around his back. "I love you, Hunter Coleburn."

When he kissed her, she felt all of his love and let it fill her heart.

Epilogue

A few days later, Hunter came home from work early.

Since the night when he'd told Eve he loved her, she'd felt like a true bride. He'd taken off work the next day, and they'd stayed in bed very late, gone out for breakfast, then returned to the house and spent the rest of the day in bed! Over the weekend, they'd sat on the patio, made love, gone for long drives and walks, then made love some more.

Now she could tell by the gleam in Hunter's eyes that he had something in mind for tonight.

"I have a surprise for you," he said.

"What is it?"

"It wouldn't be a surprise if I told you. We have to be somewhere at nine o'clock. That's all I'll say. I'm going to wear my tux, so you dress accordingly."

"And until nine o'clock?" she asked coyly.

He laughed and folded her into his arms. "Guess."

After they made tender love to each other, Hunter kissed her and went downstairs. When he returned about fifteen minutes later, he brought a tray laden with sandwiches, strawberries and baby carrots. "I don't want you to miss a meal."

He'd always taken care of her. But now his care was so much more tender, so thoroughly open. As they sat on the bed naked, eating their light supper, he told her, "Mom called today. She and Dad want us to come over for dinner on Saturday night—a family dinner. I told her I'd ask you."

"You know that's fine with me."

He kissed the tip of her nose and then studied her for a moment. "I've been thinking about something. I know how much the house in Savannah means to you. Do you want to keep it? We could spend some time there during the winter or whenever you'd like."

Her throat tightened, and she realized what a wonderful gesture Hunter was making. "Thank you for asking. But this is our home now, Hunter. This is where we'll celebrate holidays and spend time with your family. I'll always have the memories of my childhood. I'll always have treasures from my mother...and father."

"You're sure?"

She nodded. "Positive."

"I want to put this house in both of our names."

She knew that was an act of trust for him, a tangible sign that they were really husband and wife. Wrapping her arms around his neck, she gave him a long kiss until both of them realized it was time to get dressed.

Not exactly sure what Hunter had in mind for tonight, Eve chose an aqua chiffon dress from her closet.

It had a dark underslip of deep aqua, and lighter chiffon floated on top of it. With it she wore a gold locket that her father had given her when she'd turned sixteen. She fastened her hair in a French twist.

When she came out of the dressing room, Hunter was waiting for her in his tux, looking magnificently handsome, absolutely masculine. His gaze drifted over her lovingly. ''You're beautiful.''

Crossing to him, she adjusted his tie, then gave him a sweet kiss on the lips.

Less than half an hour later, Hunter drove them toward his parents' neighborhood.

''Are we going to John and Martha's?'' she asked, somewhat surprised.

''Nope.''

Puzzled, she waited, noticing each turn until she realized they were headed for the church where they'd gotten married. There was a light glowing inside.

With no other cars around, Hunter parked in front, then came around to her door and offered her his hand. She took it, and they walked hand in hand up the steps and through the church doors. When she looked inside, her breath caught.

There were candles lit in black wrought-iron holders along the pews. A small table with one large white pillar candle and two lit tapers stood in front of the altar.

She turned to Hunter.

Taking her hand, he drew her up the aisle with him, then stood with her before the altar. ''I talked to the minister about what I wanted to do tonight. At first I asked him to officiate, but he said we didn't need him.

And I think he's right. What I'd like to do is renew our wedding vows.''

He took a small black velvet box out of his pocket. Then he opened it and took out a diamond that looked like a starburst. There was one large stone in the center and smaller ones circling it. Lifting her hand, he slipped it onto her finger with her wedding band. ''I want to recommit myself to you, Eve.''

''Oh, Hunter.'' She couldn't keep her tears from spilling over.

He gently wiped them away. Then standing before the altar, he took both of her hands in his. ''You're my life, Eve. You're everything I've never had, and everything I've always wanted all rolled into one. You complete me and fill me and give me so much joy that I'm afraid sometimes. I want to ask you again to be my life partner, my lover, my friend. I promise I will love you every day as well as I possibly can. I will cherish you and always let you know I do.''

He paused for a moment, then added, ''And I will protect you and our baby for all of my days. I vow to be the best father that I can learn how to be, and to consult with you and support you as you mother our child. I will be faithful to you and share whatever I have with you as long as I live.''

Brushing away more tears, Eve smiled up at him. ''Yes, I'll be your life partner.'' She stopped to steady her voice. ''I will love you and hold you and listen to you. I've always loved you, and now I'm not afraid of loving you. I want to take care of you and our child and bring you joy and peace and all the happiness I can. You are my life, Hunter, and you are my home. I belong with you. And I promise to be faithful, to love you the best that I know how for all the rest of my life. I can't wait to mother your child, to hold your baby in my arms and know we created that life together. I vow to walk beside you through whatever life brings, to share everything I am with you, and to love you forever.''

She could see the emotion in Hunter's eyes as his arms encircled her, and he kissed her with all the promise and commitment that had filled their vows. Then he motioned to the small table. ''If we light the one large candle with our two smaller tapers, it will symbolize the two of us becoming one.''

She reached up and stroked his face. ''We *are* one now.''

They each took a single taper in their hands and together they held them to the one large candle.

It flamed high and bright, filled with the promise and hope in both of their hearts.

Hunter put his arm around her as they stared at the flame, and then he kissed her again.

They were one in love forever…for all eternity.

* * * * *

Look for Karen Rose Smith's next book,
HER HONOR-BOUND HUSBAND, on sale in
November 2000, available from Silhouette
Romance.

Look Who's Celebrating Our 20th Anniversary:

"Happy 20th birthday, Silhouette. You made the writing dream of hundreds of women a reality. You enabled us to give [women] the stories [they] wanted to read and helped us teach [them] about the power of love."

—*New York Times* bestselling author
Debbie Macomber

"I wish you continued success, Silhouette Books.... Thank you for giving me a chance to do what I love best in all the world."

—International bestselling author
Diana Palmer

"A visit to Silhouette is a guaranteed happy ending, a chance to touch magic for a little while.... It refreshes and revitalizes and makes us feel better.... I hope Silhouette goes on forever."

—Award-winning bestselling author
Marie Ferrarella

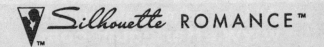

Multi-*New York Times* bestselling author

NORA ROBERTS

knew from the first how to capture readers' hearts.
Celebrate the 20th Anniversary of Silhouette Books
with this special 2-in-1 edition containing her fabulous
first book and the sensational sequel.

Coming in June

IRISH HEARTS

Adelia Cunnane's fiery temper sets proud, powerful horse
breeder Travis Grant's heart aflame and he resolves to
make this wild *Irish Thoroughbred* his own.

Erin McKinnon accepts wealthy Burke Logan's loveless
proposal, but can this ravishing *Irish Rose* win her
hard-hearted husband's love?

Also available in June from
Silhouette Special Edition (SSE #1328)

IRISH REBEL

In this brand-new sequel to *Irish Thoroughbred*, Travis and
Adelia's innocent but strong-willed daughter Keeley discovers
love in the arms of a charming Irish rogue with a talent for
horses...and romance.

Where love comes alive™

Silhouette ROMANCE™

COMING NEXT MONTH

#1456 FALLING FOR GRACE—Stella Bagwell
An Older Man
The moment Jack Barrett saw his neighbor, he wanted to know everything about her. Soon he learned beautiful Grace Holliday was pregnant and alone…and too young for him. He also found out she needed protection—from *his* jaded heart….

#1457 THE BORROWED GROOM—Judy Christenberry
The Circle K Sisters
One thing held Melissa Kennedy from her dream of running a foster home—she was single. Luckily, her sexy ranch foreman, Rob Hanson, was willing to be her counterfeit fiancé, but could Melissa keep her borrowed groom…forever?

#1458 DENIM & DIAMOND—Moyra Tarling
Kyle Masters was shocked when old friend Piper Diamond asked him to marry her. He wasn't looking for a wife, yet how could he refuse when without him, she could lose custody of her unborn child? It also didn't hurt that she was a stunning beauty….

#1459 THE MONARCH'S SON—Valerie Parv
The Carramer Crown
One minute she'd washed ashore at the feet of a prince, the next, commoner Allie Carter found herself "companion" to Lorne de Marigny's son…and falling for the brooding monarch. He claimed his heart was off-limits, yet his kisses suggested something else!

#1460 JODIE'S MAIL-ORDER MAN—Julianna Morris
Bridal Fever!
Jodie Richards was sick of seeking Mr. Right, so she decided to marry her trustworthy pen pal. But when she went to meet him, she found his brother, Donovan Masters, in his place. And with one kiss, her plan for a passionless union was in danger….

#1461 LASSOED!—Martha Shields
Pose as a model for a cologne ad? That was the *last* job champion bull-rider Tucker Reeves wanted. That is, until a bull knocked him out…and Tucker woke up to lovely photographer Cassie Burch. Could she lasso this cowboy's hardened heart for good?